THE TOMB OF THE TWELFTH IMAM

A JOAN KAHN BOOK

The Tomb of the Twelfth Imam

Richard Bulliet

HARPER & ROW, PUBLISHERS
NEW YORK, HAGERSTOWN,
SAN FRANCISCO, LONDON

FIRST EDITION

Designer: Eve Kirch

Copy editor: Margaret Cheney

Library of Congress Cataloging in Publication Data

Bulliet, Richard W
   The tomb of the twelfth imam.

   "A Joan Kahn book."
   I. Title.
PZ4.B9356To 1979   [PS3552.U44]   813'.5'4   79-1800
ISBN 0-06-010519-4

---

79 80 81 82 83 10 9 8 7 6 5 4 3 2 1

To Jack Bubon
Sayatun kam nashe

THE TOMB OF THE TWELFTH IMAM

Prologue

The feel of his father's beard touching Hossein's lips, a beard straight and coarse like the mane of the donkey he had ridden for so many days, was as real now as it had been two years before when his brother had led him to where their murdered father lay to bestow a final kiss. The feel of the beard and the smell of the rosewater his father had sprinkled it with, a smell that had been made the more distinctive by the absence of his father's breathing: these things he remembered well where so much else from that ghastly time had become a jumble.

Because he was blind he had only heard the battle between his father's few supporters, who believed his father was the Imam appointed by God as the rightful leader of all Muslims, and the army sent against them by the ruler whose illegitimate claim to power his father had bravely challenged. It had been the first battle Hossein had ever heard. The world of battles had been far removed from the pious one in which he had been reared, in the holy cities of Mecca and Medina. After all, he was poor Hossein, Hossein Makfuf, Hossein the Blind. It had been his brother Yahya who had served their father and had been his lieutenant when the day came to spread the banners of revolt across the arid plains of Iraq and Arabia. It was for Hossein to memorize the Qoran and listen to his father and brother so that in later times he could tell people how they had lived and what they had said, just as earlier pious sons had preserved the deeds and sayings of his ancestors all the way back to Ali, the son-in-law of the Prophet, upon whom be peace.

And had it not happened as God had willed? Their father had died a martyr in a grove of date palms on the banks of the Euphrates. Yahya had guided Hossein's hand to feel the arrow protruding from their father's armpit.

Then Yahya too had been made a martyr. The second battle had sounded more like a group of boys scuffling in the horse market near his teacher's house in Medina. The arrows had slain silently from ambush before a true battle could begin.

Only Hossein had been spared, spared because his blindness would prevent his father's remaining sympathizers from fixing upon him as heir to the title of Imam. So now they came to him and asked him about his father and brother, and he performed the duty he had been trained for, telling them his memories of the holy martyrs almost as if they were figures of legend whom he had never truly known.

He sometimes wondered at the things he found himself reciting: how his father had chastened sinners, what his brother had said about the end of time, and on and on. His memory was excellent for such things. He trusted it completely. Had he not memorized the Qoran before he was ten years of age? Yet the memories he dwelt on most, sometimes even while answering the questions of the faithful, were entirely different, not clear at all except for the feel of his father's beard touching his lips and the smell of rosewater. No one asked him about *these* memories. No one asked him how it had felt to ride unseeing for five weeks on a donkey through unknown country, fleeing the terrible battlefield where his father lay with the arrow in his armpit. The monotonous jolt of the donkey's tread as a guide

2

pulled it up the mountain passes out of the hot lowlands of Iraq and into the mountains of western Iran—no one asked him about *that*. The feel of escaping, blind, from a land where people spoke Arabic and could be understood to one where most of what he heard was ununderstandable Persian or Kurdish—about *that* no one asked him either.

Where the army detachment sent in pursuit had finally caught up with him he couldn't remember. Perhaps he hadn't been told. Perhaps it had been simply an overnight camp somewhere on the northern rim of the Iranian desert on the long road to the east. He had also forgotten who had been with them by that stage of their flight. The familiar voices had been left behind in the deadly date grove by the Euphrates; the new ones spoke foreign languages. Whoever they had been, they had died with Yahya in the final ambush, Yahya who had had so much to do trying to save them from capture that he had seldom spoken to him during the five weeks. Yahya had been the new Imam in the eyes of the band that had accompanied them, and God's appointed leader of the Muslim world could not be expected to spare much time for his blind brother during such a crisis. They could always talk together later, when they were safe. After the ambush, the triumphant pursuers who led Hossein on his donkey to the city of Nishapur told him that they were carrying Yahya's head with them in a covered basket. The safe times for brotherly talk were not to be.

How long would the safe times last even for Hossein himself, he wondered. It wouldn't be long now. The pious were coming in greater numbers to talk to him and to ask him questions. He filled their ears obediently as he had been trained to do, and the words that he spoke would surely not remain secret from the governor of Nishapur. The more he told to those who came, the more they came. And he told them everything, not stinting in his narration of his father's vision of the Imam coming soon to overthrow tyranny and establish the rule of peace, justice, and equality among all Muslims. This would surely come to the ears of the governor, and as surely it would lead to an inevitable

3

decision. One day soon the boy would bring Hossein rice and stew, and there would be poison in it. His death would be termed a natural one. No doubt the governor would hypocritically order an elegant tomb prepared for Hossein's remains. It didn't matter; it was all according to God's will. Even buried in this alien Iranian city far from his Arabian home, he would still retain forever the memory of his father's beard touching his lips.

The tomb was, indeed, an elegant one. It was placed in a cemetery just south of Nishapur's walls. It was understood that the governor did not look with favor upon people visiting the small building and praying at it, but some of the faithful did so anyway. For a number of years the memory of Hossein Makfuf was kept alive by those who had seen him and talked to him during the two years he had lived there after the killing of his brother. But revolution was in the air, and within a decade a new order was born and the rulers against whom Hossein's father had revolted were no more, their bones exhumed and strewn across the desert by the victors. The number of those who gave thought to the elegant little tomb of Hossein Makfuf dwindled.

Under the new regime Nishapur grew rapidly. It became a great metropolis dominating the heavily traveled caravan route that connected Baghdad, far to the west, with China and India, even farther to the east. A new grand bazaar was laid out to the northwest of the old cemetery where the tomb was located, and new cemeteries were created farther toward the edges of the expanding city. The tomb of Hossein Makfuf was gradually forgotten.

For two hundred and fifty years after the death of the blind saint the city had prospered, but the following century and a half saw recurrent episodes of riot and bloodshed between rival factions within the city and an increase in nomadic depredations without. In the end, the rioting factions and marauding nomads both had a hand in the city's destruction. Catapults

4

hurled stones and flaming balls from one quarter of the city to another as factional antagonism reached a hideous crescendo. The rival mosques and schools were burned, the bazaars looted. Again and again the nomads came to add to the destruction and pick over the remains. Disease decimated the remaining population. Finally, the metropolis was abandoned and a new, smaller Nishapur was founded on the outskirts of the old city. In a deserted cemetery in the center of a city that was itself a cemetery the tomb of Hossein Makfuf still survived in a dilapidated state.

Another century passed. Then the refounded city was itself obliterated by the invading Mongol armies of Genghiz Khan. Again it was refounded only to be destroyed three times by earthquakes. The tomb of Hossein Makfuf collapsed in the second earthquake and began to be buried by the windborne dust.

More centuries passed. A new Nishapur arose, a pale reflection of its medieval predecessor. Outside the quiet provincial town the ruins of the great metropolis were slowly buried deeper and deeper in the ground by the forces of wind and rain. Crops were planted around the mounds that had once been mosques and mansions. The tomb of Hossein Makfuf disappeared from the face of the earth.

Then after twelve hundred years the Shah decided that the ancient caravan route should be restored. A railroad should be built to bind Iran's remote eastern province of Khurasan to the heart of the new nation centered on Tehran and the cities of the west. Slowly the Shah's will was accomplished. Surveyors arrived in Nishapur and laid out a straight path for the track to follow south of the living city and eastward through the center of the broad expanse of mounds marking its dead predecessors.

The engineers followed the surveyors, and for a few months there was ample employment for everyone in the region. The dry, friable soil was broken up and carried away in baskets by scores of villagers obeying the engineers' orders to excavate a straight, level path across the land. Picks were needed in areas of the ruins where fired brick had been used for the medieval

5

buildings, but nothing was allowed to stand in the way of the surveyors' line, not even the tomb of Hossein Makfuf.

The elegant inscription was broken by the first swing of the pick at a stubborn bulge some six feet below the surface. The nearby workmen gathered around to gaze at the carved pieces as they were thrown from the trench. They could not read, nor, had they been able to read, would they have understood the alien Arabic language carved on the stone. Yet even they knew they had transgressed upon something holy. Presently a supervisor arrived to investigate the cause of the work stoppage. He could no more read the inscription than his workmen could, but he knew that the commotion it was raising had to be settled. After a brief discussion with the man who had uncovered the stone and broken it, he sent two workmen into town to fetch the mulla from the mosque and to find someone who could carve stone.

Trains came and went on the new railroad. The Nishapur station was opened with appropriate ceremony and speechmaking. As the years passed, the marvel of modern transportation became a routine sight for villagers whose lives were otherwise little changed from medieval times. Nishapur remained a quiet provincial town. Occasionally tourists came to see the alleged tomb of Omar Khayyam, but few spent the night.

One who came and stayed was a tall, craggy professor of history from the United States named Benjamin Groves. Scarcely anyone in Nishapur knew why he stayed on week after week, laboriously hiking through the mounds of ruins; but, had they known, it would have aroused little interest. The dead medieval city held no attractions for the modern inhabitants of Nishapur. If a peculiar-looking foreigner in a nylon windbreaker and long-billed baseball cap wished to waste his time building cities in his imagination, it was simply another manifestation of the abnormality of Western civilization.

From Ben Groves's point of view, being ignored was nearly ideal. One of the reasons he had been attracted to the study of

Iranian history was that there was virtually no one else active in the field. It suited him to work alone, just as it suited him to live alone both in the United States and in the dirt-cheap room (with outhouse in the courtyard) he was able to rent in one of Nishapur's minimal hostelries. The excitement of his work was sufficient for his intellectual stimulation. Chats in his rapidly improving Persian with villagers he encountered in the vicinity of the ruins satisfied his rudimentary social needs.

His project was to correlate the physical ruins with a set of aerial photographs he had winkled out of the Imperial Cartographic Bureau, the photographs to be compared in turn with textual descriptions of the old city, with the objective of drawing a hypothetical plan of medieval Nishapur. It was an almost hopeless task to make any sort of sense of the vast field of mounds and hummocks, but slowly the main features of what had once existed were taking shape in his mind. In this the conversations with villagers were sometimes helpful, but usually not. The forms of rural politeness required the exchange of a few words with whomever one encountered in the fields or on the dirt tracks that meandered from village to village.

It was just such an exchange that prompted Groves to trudge over a plowed field to look at an unusual white object on its far side near the railroad track.

"Peace be upon you," he had said to a grizzled farmer passing along the road with a rustic spade over his shoulder.

"And upon you be peace." The Arabic formula of greeting had been naturalized in Iran for over fourteen centuries.

"Do you know what the white thing is over there?"

"Tomb."

"Whose tomb?"

"God knows." The expression was uttered in piety.

"Is it old?"

"God knows."

The man passed on, leaving the exasperated foreigner no choice but to look for himself. When he reached the object, he saw that it was a plaster pillar not much larger than a fire hydrant with a carved stone set in one side. The carving was quite crude, but the inscription began clearly enough: "This is the resting place of the late Hossein Makfuf. . . ." Groves extracted a ballpoint pen and a folded piece of graph paper from the pocket of his windbreaker and began to copy the clumsy letters as accurately as possible.

Sha' ban: The First Month

CHAPTER 1

A slender manicured finger reached out in the dark and traced the faint yellow profile produced by an intrusive beam of street lighting outlining a man's lean, muscled torso seated upright on the bed.

"Can't you sleep, Mohammad?" There was no reply. "Didn't you have a good time?" The man's flank was still wet with perspiration. He reached for her hand and folded it in his own. The light from the street turned her long blond hair into a golden halo around the shadowed face.

"A wonderful time," he said. "I was just preoccupied with wondering what I would do differently if I were the Shah. It was a silly thought."

"What did you decide? Anything special?"

"No, I suppose not. It's just that there are so many administrative logjams and so much waste. Sometimes I think the Shah has grand plans but just doesn't understand how to put them into effect." He reclined again in the soft alcove she made for him at her side.

"You don't have to leave for another two hours," she said tentatively. In answer his hand reached across her body and began a slow descent.

As Minister of Culture and Art Mohammad Hormozi merited three deputy ministers, a dozen general directors, four tiers of secretaries safeguarding the door to his office, and the ministerial office itself, of palatial proportions, dominated by an immense cream-colored Kirman carpet with an exquisitely intricate central medallion of blue and pink flowers. Nevertheless, the announcement from his private secretary that a full colonel from SAVAK was waiting to see the minister was sufficient to cause even this most secure government official to cast his mind back over any seditious or disloyal thoughts he might ever have entertained. It was unlikely, of course, that the secret police officer's business would concern Hormozi personally, but a few sentences spoken to his mistress in the dead of night weighed uncomfortably in his memory as the door opened to admit the colonel.

Colonel Rahmatollah Ziya was much older than Hormozi had envisioned, and he had a suspicion, as they shook hands and exchanged formal greetings, that the white-haired officer felt that Hormozi looked too young and robust at forty-two to be a cabinet minister. The thought served to calm the minister's apprehensions. Iran is a country for young men, he thought. The older generation must give way to the young who have the modern training and the determination to transform the nation. The very formality and circuitousness with which the SAVAK officer approached the subject of his visit was a symptom of the medieval mentality of old Iran that must be discarded.

"I would be interested in knowing what determination Your Excellency has reached about the matter of the tombstone." The colonel's courtly manner went well with his ornate uniform. He seated himself on a Louis Quinze sofa.

"*Will* reach, Colonel," Hormozi said. "The determination has not yet been made. The Imperial Historical Society will give its report soon to the High Council on Culture and Art. The head of the council reports to the Deputy Minister for Culture, and he reports to me. I will consult with the Minister of Information and the Director of the Religious Endowment Authority before formulating a decision, which I will then submit to the Prime Minister. Naturally, this all takes time. A decision of religious importance cannot be taken lightly, however."

A sigh rippled Colonel Ziya's unfashionably long white mustaches. "You are informed, Your Excellency, that it is the wish of His Imperial Majesty that the tombstone be found to be fraudulent? You are aware of this wish?"

The minister nodded. "Of course. I was simply describing the process by which His Majesty's insight will, in all probability, be confirmed by the Ministry of Culture and Art."

Colonel Ziya waved the precisely worded reply aside. "His Majesty's insight is not in this instance to be found correct. When you have received reports in the manner you described, they must verify the genuineness of the tombstone. You will keep this finding a secret, of course, until appropriate formal announcement can be made; but you should not keep it a secret too successfully."

The minister was visibly troubled. The Shah's wishes had never before, in Hormozi's experience, been countermanded by SAVAK, his secret police organization. "You will excuse me for appearing confused, colonel, but I am uncertain how to interpret what you have just said. It is by no means a secret that His Imperial Majesty suspects the stone to be a forgery. Knowledgeable people expect this suspicion to be confirmed. Only the devotees of the cult of Hossein Makfuf believe the stone is genuine."

Colonel Ziya leaned his large body forward. "That is true, Your Excellency. But we are dealing here with a matter of national security."

Hormozi's dense black eyebrows asked a question.

"That is correct," answered the colonel. "A matter of security. Let me be very blunt. There are people who seek to overthrow the government and depose His Imperial Majesty. We know who some of them are; others we don't know. Nor do we know exactly what they plan to do. Our best informant unfortunately died before he told us very much—if, in fact, he knew very much. It is sufficient for you to know that an announcement that the tombstone is a forgery could force them to alter their plans and thus prevent us from learning what we need to know about the conspiracy. That is why we wish them to find out that the opposite decision is being reached."

"But what possible connection could that absurd stone have with a plot against His Imperial Majesty?" the minister asked.

"When I hear you speak of religion over the radio, Your Excellency, I sense that you are one of Iran's most profound Muslim thinkers. Your philosophy of being a true Muslim while still being a man of the modern world is very encouraging, even to a man of an older generation, such as myself, who was born in a different age. There are too few of the younger generation who understand the harmony of Islam and the modern world as you do. That is why I know you will not laugh, Your Excellency, when I tell you that the one who seeks to overthrow His Imperial Majesty calls himself the Twelfth Imam. Religion and politics: it's a dangerous combination."

Hormozi smiled slightly. "I thank you for confiding in me, Colonel Ziya." He was about to ask for further elucidation of the portentous disclosure when his visitor abruptly rose. The leavetaking was as formal as the greeting had been. After ushering the colonel out, Abbas Azad, the minister's gaunt, hawk-nosed private secretary, informed his chief that the automobile was waiting to take him to the reception being given for the new American ambassador.

As was so often the case, Tehran's crushing traffic congestion gave Mohammad Hormozi ample time for thinking within the silent upholstered cocoon of his Mercedes. He recalled his earlier anxiety over the remarks he had made to his mistress. He needn't have been so concerned, and to the best of his recollection he had said nothing really bad about the Shah anyway. As

14

he reflected on his misplaced fears, he congratulated himself on not choosing Iranian women as mistresses. The chances of SAVAK's hearing of an indiscretion were so much less with foreign women. Nevertheless, he should train himself to be more careful. The next colonel to knock on his door might have a more serious mission.

Above the din of the reception for the ambassador, an introduction was made by the program director of the Iran-America Society, a striking woman of thirty-five with long silky hair who stood out among the elegantly dressed and coiffed Iranian and American women by reason of her extreme blondness.

"Dr. Mohammad Hormozi, may I present Professor Benjamin Groves? Professor Groves is with us this year on an NEH senior scholars grant."

"How pleased I am to meet you, Professor Groves."

"Dr. Hormozi," responded the tall, craggy American with a stilted attempt at a bow.

"I specifically asked Miss Bengston to introduce us because . . ."

"We've met before, I believe."

"We have?" Hormozi asked.

"Three years ago. You were making a lecture tour in the States. In point of fact, I introduced you when you came to speak in Chicago. Of course, you weren't Minister of Culture and Art then."

Hormozi beamed. "Of course. Now, I remember distinctly. It was silly of me to forget. It was at the University of Chicago."

"Northwestern University," muttered the professor.

"But at that time I was totally unaware of your discovery of the Hossein Makfuf tombstone." Groves suppressed a desire to point out that he had published the tombstone inscription a good two years before Hormozi's Chicago lecture. "As you must surely know, Professor Groves, it has fallen to my ministry to make an official determination regarding the genuineness of the stone. We are studying it from all points of view, naturally, but confidentially you may be interested to know that some of our most knowledgeable people are inclined to accept its validity." That should satisfy Colonel Ziya's desire for ill-concealed secrecy, thought the minister. "But you have thought about the problem longer than any of us have. What's your opinion?"

Groves eyed the dapper official with the slightly receding black hair skeptically. "My opinion has been a matter of public record for at least five years. If you aren't familiar with it, I will be happy to send you a copy of my article."

"Yes, but that was your opinion five years ago. Opinions have a way of changing. I'm interested in knowing what your opinion is now, today."

"I assure you, Dr. Hormozi, that it is the same now as it was when I published my article describing the stone. It is hardly a matter I would change my mind on. When you consider that Iran's third-largest city grew up around the tomb of a saint who was seven generations removed from the Prophet Mohammad and the tomb of the man's sister gave rise to the tenth-largest city, it's no small matter to discover the tomb of a cousin who lived almost a century earlier and was two generations closer to the Prophet. I considered the matter for a number of years before deciding to put my discovery in print, and I obviously wouldn't have done it if I'd intended to change my mind about the tombstone's being real."

Hormozi's trim black mustache accentuated the whiteness of his teeth when he flashed a smile, this time accompanied by a wink. "I most certainly appreciate all of that, Professor Groves; but a less scrupulous person than yourself might have taken a gamble just for the notice it would arouse."

"Are you suggesting . . ."

"Not at all. As I said, some of our top historians here in Iran seem inclined to agree with your judgment. I only . . ."

"Let me tell you something, Hormozi," Groves said testily. "I once read a very stupid novel by Sax Rohmer called *The Mask of Fu Manchu.* I recommend it to you if you like reading racist, imperialist thrillers. In it the mask once worn by an early Mus-

16

lim religious revolutionary is discovered by a British archaeologist and then stolen by the evil genius Dr. Fu Manchu, who wants to use it to inspire religious fanaticism in the hearts of the world's Muslims, thus prompting them to throw off the domination of the white men. Needless to say, in the novel intrepid British heroes foil the plot. It's really a very ridiculous book, but it has a moral to it that I happen to agree with: Don't go meddling with other people's religious traditions if you're not prepared to deal with the consequences. What I wrote about the tombstone of Hossein Makfuf is my final opinion, and I will stand by it."

The minister watched the professor's gray herringbone suit disappear past a bouquet of colorful frocks clustered around the non-alcoholic punch bowl. "Sensitive, isn't he?" Hormozi thought.

Susan Bengston, with the long blond hair, had come up and covertly entwined her arm in his. "I don't think he likes you, Mohammad."

"Well, no reason why he should. I don't like him much either. American professors are a depressing bunch. Petty, pedantic bores endlessly concerned with faculty politics. That's one thing I learned from studying in the United States—it may even be the only thing."

Susan Bengston looked up at him. "Are you saying that to get my goat?"

Hormozi grinned and whispered in her ear, "I didn't know there was any part of you I hadn't had yet."

CHAPTER 2

Amidst the hurly-burly of haggling, chadur-shrouded women and the chaos of gesticulating tradesmen that packed the covered bazaar of Arak, Jamshid Ansari strolled the central passage with studied deliberation and apparent calm. He did not often visit minor provincial cities, even those within a hundred and fifty kilometers of the Iranian capital such as Arak. Consequently, his close attention to the array of goods displayed in the long rows of small open storefronts afforded something more than a convenient excuse to look back and see if he was being followed. It was also a chance to see vestiges of the Iranian past that were becoming increasingly rare in Tehran. Visible across well-trodden thresholds to the side of the central passage were covered courtyards enclosed by two-story brick arcades screening small rooms that served as warehouses. Worn and dilapidated but impressive in the geometry of their ornamental brickwork and the sophistication of their elaborate domes, the structures reminded the young man that once Iran had been a great and respected country, as it would be again with the inspired and humane leadership the revolution would bring.

Past the shiny aluminum-ware shops, which he surmised would have been producing artistically chased and inlaid bronze utensils a century before, he made a sharp turn into a darker, less crowded alleyway. From beyond a row of stalls selling ropes and cords he heard a rhythmic chanting and drumming that steadily increased as he sauntered along. The sound emanated from a loudspeaker over a small doorway above which was a green plaque identifying it as the entrance to the Imam Reza House of Strength of Arak. Confident that to a casual bystander his pinstripe suit and wide silk tie would mark him as a big-city tourist interested in quaint old customs of the traditional athletic clubs, Jamshid stooped and went through the door.

Beneath the lofty parabola of a brick dome was a circular room in the center of which was a circular pit approximately one meter deep and three meters across. Standing with legs spread and braced against the inside wall of the pit were eight stocky men and teenaged boys, barefoot and shirtless, wearing embroidered red breeches that cinched just below the knee. In the center of the circle a gnarled older man led them in calisthenic exercises to the beat of the drum and the rhythmic chanting. The drummer-chanter was seated in an open alcove set in the wall a few feet above the short passageway that led in from the bazaar. Clad like the men in the pit and dripping with perspiration, he had before him a new-looking microphone that amplified his chanting and drumming to an almost deafening extent. At his side was a shallow bronze brazier filled with hot coals upon which he occasionally threw a small amount of some kind of herb that gave the air in the high room a distinctive sweet aroma.

Although, like any Iranian, Jamshid was well aware of his country's ancient tradition of zurkhanehs, or houses of strength, he had previously seen only staged performances in Tehran and had never before witnessed the daily, routine exercises. He was late for his meeting, but he was perfectly content to wait and watch for a pause. Then Jamshid went to the alcove and said a few words to the drummer, who nodded him toward a low archway on the opposite side of the circle, where there was an inner room. The drumming resumed as he made his way behind the backs of the athletes.

The inner room was smaller and was evidently designed for changing clothes and storing equipment. Jamshid recognized only one of the six men who looked his way as he entered. As the outspoken rector of the Ja'fari Islamic Law College in the nearby holy city of Qom, Ayatollah Pirzadeh was a frequently photographed public figure. He was wearing the tight white turban, white gown, and open brown robe that comprised the uniform of Iran's mullas, or Muslim clergy. Also in keeping with clerical style was his full black beard, trimmed to a uniform half-inch length. Thick black glasses frames completed the austere image.

"I am Jamshid Ansari," said the late arrival.

"I recognize you from your photograph," replied the mulla. "You know who I am. You need not know the names of the others."

Jamshid glanced briefly at the faces of the other five men, who looked much like the ones in the exercise circle, and found a spot to sit on the brick floor between two of them. "I apologize for being late. The bus from Tehran was delayed by a highway accident, and I had to be sure I was not being followed."

"You were not followed," said the mulla. "If you had been, we would have been warned well before you reached the zurkhaneh. Things do not go unnoticed in small cities. That is why I preferred to meet here rather than in Tehran or Qom."

Jamshid was conscious that the five other men were all looking at him. He felt as if he were being scrutinized for some hidden defect. From their rough hands, skullcap haircuts, and cheap blue suits he judged them to be members of the working class. He could feel that they regarded him as an outsider, a pampered intellectual; but he consoled himself with the thought that they had no reason to think otherwise since they probably understood little or nothing of his political philosophy.

When the scrutiny seemed to be completed, the bearded mulla resumed speaking. "The fact that you have come tells us that your people have accepted our offer to join us." Jamshid began to nod agreement. The mulla raised his hand. "Before you say anything, there is something I wish you to witness."

One of the men quietly left the room and returned in a few moments with a heavily muscled young man in red breeches still sweating from the exercises. Ayatollah Pirzadeh looked up at the heavily breathing athlete with a gaze that seemed full of beatitude.

"Reza Forughi," he intoned as if reading a name from the heavenly scroll, "we know that you are a good and a pious man. We also know that despite hard work you are a poor man with many needs you cannot meet. It is cruel that we live in a corrupt world where the poor are so badly treated while the rich steal the nation's wealth. But we also know, Reza Forughi, that you have been paid one thousand tomans by SAVAK to report to them about meetings that take place in this building." The regular heaving of the young man's chest suddenly halted. "What I could do, Reza, is allow you to keep the one thousand tomans and give you false and misleading information to convey to the Shah's police spies. But how could I be certain that your devotion to the Twelfth Imam would not weaken again in the future? The Twelfth Imam demands loyalty."

The mulla lowered his eyes and began to whisper a prayer. Reza Forughi opened his mouth to speak, but nothing came out because at the same instant the man who had ushered him into the room tossed a loop of fine wire over his head and pulled it tight, with his knee in the young man's back. Jamshid struggled to control his surging stomach and appear as calm as the others as they watched the dying athlete jerking against the lethal wire.

When the two breeches-clad athletes summoned to remove

the body had done their job, never showing the slightest sign that the corpse was that of their fellow club member, Pirzadeh turned his attention once again to Jamshid.

"Let me tell you why I forced you to witness that unfortunate occurrence before you said anything further. You are about to make a commitment on behalf of the Muslim Marxist Alliance to support the violent overthrow of the corrupt government of the Shah of Iran and the creation of a new revolutionary government under the Twelfth Imam. I wanted you to realize in the fullest way what this commitment means. Your people must play their assigned role without hesitation or second thoughts. They must be as loyal in carrying out your orders as my men are in carrying out mine. Furthermore, I wanted to impress upon you that our knowledge of what SAVAK is doing is far greater than SAVAK's knowledge of what we are doing. The corollary of this is that if your group has been penetrated by SAVAK, or comes to be penetrated, we shall surely learn of it and punish the traitor. You must convey this warning to your group when you return to Tehran."

Jamshid summoned up a properly disdainful tone in which to reply. "We are not mere amateurs playing at student politics, Ayatollah Pirzadeh. Our central committee has decided to accept your leadership in the revolution. It understands and accepts the risks. I can also assure you that we have our own ways of uncovering and dealing with informers. We have only taken this step, however, on your assurance that in the formation of the government after the revolution our voice will be heard. We shall fight with you as devout Muslims, but we shall be fighting also as the vanguard of the oppressed workers and peasants of Iran."

The mulla bowed his head until his black beard touched his gown. "I repeat to you my assurance that you will have such a role. The government of the Twelfth Imam will be just and humane and will ensure equality among all true believers."

"Then we are with you."

"God be praised. The manifestation of the Twelfth Imam

shall occur in the month of Moharram, six months from now. The place and the exact timing will be communicated to you when it becomes necessary for you to know them. For the time being you have three missions. The first is to forge an alliance with the Communist underground and other radical groups and to secure either their allegiance or their neutrality. Do not divulge my name or the timing of the revolution. Otherwise, you may make them whatever promises are necessary to gain their cooperation. But remember this: we shall never grant a share of power to any atheist Communists, only to true Muslims. The second mission is to communicate with the Soviet Union and sound out its reaction to a possible change of government. The third is to acquire the materials on a list I shall convey to you after you have returned to Tehran. These items must be acquired through the Soviet Union. Other possible sources are not acceptable. When you receive them, you will contact me for further instructions. Is all of this clear?"

"Quite clear. The missions are not beyond our abilities."

"Then you may leave."

"May I ask one question?" The mulla nodded permission. "Who is the Twelfth Imam? Is it you?"

Ayatollah Pirzadeh gazed at Jamshid with the same beatitudinous look he had visited upon the doomed informer. "No, I am not the Twelfth Imam. I have never met him. Since you are interested, however, I can tell you that he will enter Iranian territory within the next week. Now you may leave."

When Jamshid had departed, one of the anonymous men left in the room commented, "He was frightened."

An unaccustomed-looking smile broke the mulla's dark visage. "We must keep him frightened. His kind cannot be trusted if they are given too much opportunity to think things through clearly."

CHAPTER 3

Five days later a blind man about forty years of age, dressed as a mulla and using a thick, gnarled staff as a guide, was cleared through Iranian passport control at the Iraqi border near Khorramshahr. He accepted gifts of food from pious Muslims moved by his saintly demeanor but disdained offers of transportation and set off walking after a day's rest on the long road northward toward Qom. His sightless eyes were on the distant horizon, and his mind was filled with thoughts of that glorious day when God would restore his vision and charge him with his mission.

On that same day a blue Ford van jounced to the end of four hundred kilometers of torture over washboard gravel and relaxed onto the quiet smoothness of an asphalt highway in northeastern Iran. The sighs of relief that filled the van came from Professor Benjamin Groves and the porcine, red-faced driver, Freddy Desuze, economic attaché with the American embassy. The sighs quickly gave way to whining music emanating from an exotic-looking portable short-wave radio resting on the bench seat behind the front bucket seats. A few more kilometers clicked by, and the monotonous drone of the mournful violin solo gave way to a well-modulated female voice announcing in Persian the start of a program on religious values featuring the Minister of Culture and Art, Dr. Mohammad Hormozi.

"Oh, Christ," said Groves with disgust, "that's all we need. For two days this heap rattles so much it's hardly worth listening; then, as soon as we get a little quiet, that hypocrite comes on."

"Not fond of the distinguished Minister of Culture and Art?" asked Freddy Desuze, an ironic smirk spreading over his pudgy face.

"Opportunistic demagogue, that's what he is. Do you know him?"

"Met him for the first time at that party for Ambassador Dermott where I ran into you. I gather you know him from some time back, though."

"Mostly by reputation. I met him once or twice in the States, but his reputation alone is enough to make you hate him. Personally, he's charming, I suppose, at least to people he wants to cultivate; but his way of advancing himself is disgusting. He has a degree in physics or something like that from Caltech. So he makes himself out to be a Western-educated scientist. At the same time, he passes himself off as a great Islamic philosopher. Manages to play both ends against the middle. His books on Islam, which are okay but nothing special, are accepted as masterpieces in Europe and the U.S. because everyone is impressed that a Western scientist can be a profound and devout Muslim —which, by the way, he isn't. Turn the situation around and he's regarded as a guru in this country because everyone is so impressed that a profound and devout Muslim can also be a Western-trained scientist. He has an almost fanatic following among college students and gives radio sermons at every opportunity. Moreover, he's six years younger than I am and already a cabinet minister."

"Sounds like quite a fellow. You're not just jealous of him, are you?" Groves snorted and stared at the barren landscape. "I mean, it sounds like some successful books, a bunch of followers among college students, and being cultural overlord for the whole damn country is the sort of thing someone in your trade might kind of like." Freddy Desuze's voice had a hint of a drawl in it.

Groves smiled slightly. "I guess it would be a nice spot to be in. You want to know how many copies my last book sold in the first year? Five hundred even. Four hundred and seventy-two at the library discount rate and twenty-eight to the eager public. My total earnings will be about a thousand dollars over six years; then it will be remaindered, and that will be the end of it." Groves seemed to be speaking more to himself than to the driver.

After a few more minutes listening to the radio harangue, Groves reached back and turned it off. They were now at the top of the pass, and the flat arid bowl of the Nishapur plain stretched out below them. It was a uniform beige following the fall harvest of wheat and cotton.

"Of course I'm jealous of Hormozi," the professor added as they descended. "When we met at that party last week, he didn't even remember me. He also implied that I was some kind of sensation seeker because of my publication of the Hossein Makfuf tombstone. Talk about the pot calling the kettle black. If he could think of a way to do it, he'd try to make himself Shah."

"Who wouldn't?" Freddy said. To the left between the highway and the low mountains that fringed the northern side of the Nishapur bowl they were passing the first village on the plain, a collection of low domed adobe buildings presenting a continuous, featureless wall to the outside world, pierced only by a single dirt track that angled toward the highway. "You've mentioned this tombstone of somebody or other before. What's that all about?"

"Our third day on the road and you finally get around to asking me what I'm doing here. Not a very inquisitive sort, are you, Freddy?"

"Oh, I'm inquisitive enough. It's just that you asked about my business first after we left Tehran, and it took me two whole days to tell you about it. I figure we have another half hour before we get to Nishapur. That should be plenty of time for you to tell me about your business before I let you off." The rotund driver looked over at his gangly passenger and winked.

Groves had observed the rule that nonpaying passengers don't bore their hosts with their life stories until invited to. Now he searched for an explanation of his work that a fat economist could understand.

"Okay. There was this guy who lived over twelve hundred years ago. He was important because he was the great-grandson of Ali, the son-in-law of the Prophet Mohammad."

"And his name was Hossein whoever?"

"No. Just wait. It's Ali who is at the center of Iranian religion. The Iranians, as Muslims, follow Mohammad as a prophet; but their branch of Islam really goes bananas over Mohammad's son-in-law Ali and his family. Ali was also Mohammad's first cousin, but don't worry about that. Okay. This Ali had a great-grandson who led a big revolt in Iraq back around A.D. 740. He wanted to become the leader of Islam. It didn't work. The revolt was put down, and the great-grandson was killed. But he had several sons, one of whom fled out here after the revolt and was hunted down and killed. The others the history books are a little vague about, and one of those others was a blind fellow named Hossein. The Arabic word for blind is *makfuf;* so he's called Hossein Makfuf: Hossein the Blind."

"And that's the one whose tombstone you found?"

"That's the one whose tombstone I found."

"And?"

"Well, first, finding the tomb of somebody like that is like finding the false teeth of John the Baptist. It can be really important in religious terms. Even though Hossein Makfuf isn't that important historically, he's the earliest member of the Iranians' holy family to have a known burial site here in Iran. Since tombs of holy figures like him usually become pilgrimage sites, a regular cult of Hossein Makfuf sprang up from nowhere after I published my article. It started slowly, but this last year it's really taken off. Nishapur is about to become an important pilgrimage center. That's the reason I've come back: to study the growth of the Hossein Makfuf cult. No telling where it might end. It could be the biggest thing to hit Iranian religion in a hundred years."

"And what's second?"

"Second, there's a dispute over whether the tombstone is genuine or not."

"Why's that?"

"Because when I found it twelve years ago I thought the date on it was absurdly early. It was a newly cut stone preserving a twelve-hundred-year-old inscription."

"And the original inscription is gone?"

"Entirely."

"What about the tomb itself?"

"There isn't any. Just the stone."

"Sounds like a forgery." Groves didn't reply. "I mean, if finding a tomb like that could mean a new pilgrimage center, then whoever owns the property the tomb is on is going to get rich. It just stands to reason that it's a forgery."

"The possibility of a forgery has been mentioned," said the professor coldly.

"You could even have done it yourself if you wanted to get famous." Freddy glanced over to see a nettled expression on his passenger's leathery face.

"That's what Hormozi suggested. But the fact of the matter is that I didn't forge it, and I'm sure it's not a forgery."

"Why's that?"

"Because it's too incompetently made to be a forgery. The stone is badly carved; there are mistakes in spelling and language; it mixes up Arabic and Persian words. It's a mess. Only an idiot would take it for a genuine medieval stone." Freddy eyed him quizzically as they passed the first houses on the outskirts of Nishapur. "I have a lovely theory to explain how it came to be carved."

"Yeah, well, some other time, professor. If I get too fascinated by the theory, I might run down one of those sheep over there and never get you to that education office you said you wanted to be dropped at."

The education office, when found, proved to be located in the new cream-colored brick building of the Ministry of Culture and Art near the intersection of two broad but lightly trafficked avenues which marked the center of Nishapur. The avenues had been cut in straight lines perpendicular to each other through the heart of the old city forty years before, at a time when there were virtually no motor vehicles in the whole northeastern province of Khurasan. In the intervening decades they had slowly become lined with banks, official buildings, and a few small modern stores, while the preponderance of commercial establishments remained in the winding covered bazaar that was cut in two by one of the new avenues just east of the central intersection.

The dress of the men in the Ministry of Culture and Art building was entirely in the modern mode, unlike what could still be commonly seen in the bazaar, but the exaggerated deference and formality with which Groves was greeted and ushered to the office of the Chief of Education perpetuated a pattern of etiquette many centuries old. As Groves remembered from his last visit to Nishapur a dozen years before, the Chief of Education's spacious office was well supplied with silent petitioners, seated or standing, waiting to be noticed by the chief so that they could transact their bit of business. Rank rather than time spent waiting would determine the order in which they would be noticed, and Groves's own high rank was immediately indicated by his being directed to a chair next to the chief's desk.

Rapidly dispatching with a flourish of signatures the business he was engaged in, the chief turned his full attention to his American visitor. The welcome was profuse, and the inevitable tea was ordered. The old chief, whom Groves had known before, had long since been reassigned elsewhere; the new chief, named Ebrahim Borumand, was a small dark man with unusually dense facial hair that made him look quite unshaven although it was only two in the afternoon. From previous hard-earned experience, Groves knew the right technique to ingratiate himself with Iranian officials, and he proceeded to praise, in his most extravagant Persian vocabulary, the evident modernization Nishapur had undergone, in which, he implied, Mr. Ebrahim Borumand had surely played a leading role. For his part, the chief expressed his pleasure at meeting the man responsible for the new pilgrimage site that showed promise of bringing business and activity to the dreary provincial city. At the same time, he made a point of indicating that, until the Ministry of Culture and Art ruled on the genuineness of the tomb of Hossein Makfuf, as an employee of the Ministry he could make no formal recognition of its existence. Until then, his assistance to Professor Groves's research would have to be of an informal character.

Since through prior correspondence with the ministry in Tehran Groves had gained the necessary permits to carry on his study and had been assured that lodgings would be found for him during his stay, there was no further assistance he needed. All that remained to be done after his formal courtesy call upon the chief was to find out whether his earlier-than-scheduled arrival, the product of his chance meeting with Freddy Desuze, would cause problems with his living arrangements. But there was no problem, and soon he was ensconced in the tiny spare room of a high-school English teacher named Mahmud Kamel, who had offered his hospitality, as was immediately apparent, as a way of having a captive American to practice his English on.

"It is too much an honor that you live here," said Mr. Kamel politely as he ladled a fluffy mountain of rice onto Groves's plate at dinner. Mrs. Kamel being excluded for reasons of propriety from eating with the foreign guest, Groves had no alternative but to devote all of his attention to the eager teacher.

CHAPTER **4**

Far below the gilded splendor of the great bulbous dome atop the shrine mosque of Fatima in the holy city of Qom, on an unusually warm fall day, Mohammad Hormozi in meticulous white suit, white tie, and white shoes was taking pains to be on time for an appointment in an environment where time was seldom hurried. Between the two towering wooden pillars that flanked the tall rectangular entrance to the mosque itself, he slipped out of his shoes and into a pair of large floppy slippers supplied for the worshipers. The sanctuary of the mosque was almost entirely covered by large carpets, whose deep colors gave a jewel-like glow when struck by the occasional ray of light from the small windows high on the barrel of the dome. Needing no directions, Hormozi strode diagonally across the sanctified space, passed to the right of the high, narrow wooden pulpit, and climbed a well-worn flight of stone steps leading up from a scarcely noticeable doorway. The small anteroom at the top of the stairs was deserted. He tapped gently on the ancient double-leaved wooden door, then without waiting for a re-

31

sponse he opened the door a crack and peered inside. The white-bearded elder sitting cross-legged at the far side of the small room nodded slightly in his direction. Hormozi slipped quietly into the room and stood silently just inside the door.

A group of very young men clad in the turbans and robes of mullas rose and one by one kissed the hand of their ancient mentor before withdrawing from the room past the waiting visitor. Hormozi surveyed the familiar surroundings while he waited. Had it not been for the iron-willed determination of a wealthy uncle wedded to modern ways, he might have continued his early training in the mosque school, eventually become a mulla, and perhaps, in time, risen to the spiritual heights of the blessed Ayatollah Shirazi who was about to receive him in audience. Secretly he felt that being the paramount religious dignitary of the holy shrine of Fatima at Qom was a far greater honor than being Minister of Culture and Art; and he would have admitted publicly that his own spacious modern office paled to insignificance beside this small room, with its walls and ceiling covered with cobalt-blue Kashan tiles bearing in the most intricate calligraphy dozens of verses from the holy Qoran. In his heart, however, he knew that his own ambition and worldly tastes would always have prevented him from sitting where the humble, saintly Ayatollah Shirazi was now sitting to receive him.

He kissed the soft wrinkled hand and seated himself on a simple mat facing an identical one on which the bright-eyed old mulla was sitting. The stone floor was all too palpable through the thin rush mat.

After a slow, formal exchange of pious expressions of greeting and deference, Hormozi was finally able to state his mission. "I have come, Reverend Sir, to inquire about Hossein Makfuf."

The old man's voice was quiet but with an unexpected grating, rasping quality. "We have found in our libraries no proof that Hossein Makfuf was not buried in Nishapur, and no proof that he was."

"And what opinion have the learned mullas arrived at?"

"If the stone marks the true tomb of Hossein Makfuf," rasped the elder, "its discovery is a miracle from God. A miracle. Miracles are not common, but it is possible that we have been blessed by being alive when one has occurred."

Hormozi waited to see if there was more. Ayatollah Shirazi said no more. So Hormozi continued: "With regard to the theory of the American, Professor Benjamin Groves, have the mullas reached an opinion? You will recall, reverend sir, that Professor Groves noted that the tombstone was located in a field quite near the excavation made for the railroad to pass through the ruins of the old city of Nishapur. He theorized that the digging of the railroad may have destroyed the original tomb and that the engineers may have had some of the information on the original, broken tombstone carved on a new stone to protect themselves if any report was made that they had destroyed an important antiquity. He reasoned that they did not report the discovery themselves because it would certainly have halted, at least temporarily, further work on the railroad. Has this theory been studied, Reverend Sir?"

The mulla's eyes were bright, expressionless dots surrounded by wrinkles between the luxuriant white beard and the equally white turban. "If the stone marks the true tomb of Hossein Makfuf, its discovery is a miracle," he repeated.

"I am most humbly grateful for your opinion," said the Minister of Culture and Art respectfully. "Perhaps you could tell me one additional thing," he added as if by afterthought. "In principle, could there be any connection between Hossein Makfuf and the Twelfth Imam?"

Ayatollah Shirazi snorted loudly and derisively. "You seem to have forgotten what you learned while you were with us, Mohammad Hormozi." His voice was louder and was even more grating. "The Twelfth Imam was Mohammad Mahdi, who disappeared from the eyes of men in the year 879 and whose return will mark the world's entry into the era of God's perfect rule. Not only was the Twelfth Imam a different person from Hossein Makfuf, living in a different century, but the returned

Mahdi could never be suffering the defect of blindness. He will be a perfect man come to perfect the world of men. I cannot believe, Mohammad Hormozi, that you are truly ignorant of these matters. They are most elementary."

Hormozi felt at a loss for words. Finally he managed to say, "Forgive my ignorance, Reverend Sir. I was confused by something that was recently told to me."

"I have heard your confusions on the radio." The white-bearded mulla now sounded quite irritated. "You say many things that are not true about our religion. It would be better if you left these matters to those of us who are free from such errors."

Hormozi was rescued from his momentary loss of composure by the very bitterness of the mulla's words. "As you are aware, Reverend Sir," he replied with a bite in his own words, "the organization of our state under the far-seeing guidance of His Imperial Majesty empowers me to instruct the people on matters of religion. While we respect and seek out the opinion of the religious authorities, we are no longer in the dark ages when theirs was the sole opinion that mattered."

With this he rose and quickly bent to give the slightest kiss to the elder's hand. He backed out of the room deferentially but a bit too quickly for proper etiquette. As he turned around just outside the low wooden door, he came face to face in the small anteroom with a vaguely familiar middle-aged mulla wearing a close-cropped black beard and glasses with heavy black frames. He stepped quickly by him and disappeared down the stone stairway. Ayatollah Pirzadeh watched him depart and then stooped slightly to enter the small blue room.

Pirzadeh spoke as soon as he had shut the door. "I fear it is a mistake to involve that man. He is not stupid."

"That is why we must involve him, Pirzadeh," came the rasped reply. "He is clever, and he has a following among the young. If we do not destroy his power now while it is still weak, we may not be able to do so as easily in the future. Besides, if he decided to denounce the tombstone, it could interfere with the pilgrimage."

"But will we succeed in destroying him? The consequences of failure could be costly."

The old eyes that had previously seemed expressionless now took on a malicious glint. "We can trust Colonel Ziya to ensure that the investigation casts a broad enough net to envelop him. When the revolt of our Twelfth Imam is suppressed and SAVAK discovers a vast conspiracy of godless Communists, Soviet infiltration, and Iraqi subversion, the man who, contrary to the Shah's will, certified the validity of the tombstone will inevitably be taken for an enemy of the Shah. He will fall with all the others."

"But can we be sure that the investigation will reveal nothing of our hand in the matter? Colonel Ziya cannot control everything."

"Nothing will go wrong. Take heart. Nothing will go wrong. We communicate only with the deluded Marxist Ansari. Even if he survives the event and tries to save himself by confession, we shall simply reply that it was we who unmasked the false Twelfth Imam and saved the throne. Who will the Shah believe: us or the Communist? No, Pirzadeh, when this is finished, those who would pervert the faith with communism will be dead, and we shall be glorified as the saviors of the Shah. What choice will he have but to reward us and accept our advice? He will have been warned that the next time we could tip the balance against him."

"The next time?"

The ancient mulla gave an eerie cackle. "When the true Twelfth Imam returns. When the Mahdi comes to destroy the Shah."

Ramadan: The Second Month

National Security Advisor Emmanuel Holachek looked up at the sound of his door opening to see his special assistant for Middle Eastern affairs, Bill Keller, coming into the office. The young, studious-looking special assistant was a familiar figure, and the tedious inevitability of Middle Eastern crises entitled him to unannounced visits to his boss's office.

"Who is it this time, the Arabs or the Israelis?"

"Surprise, surprise! Neither one."

The National Security Advisor closed his small, oriental-looking eyes and sighed, half with relief and half with apprehension. The Arabs and Israelis could be depended upon to raise the most dangerous problems, but the other countries of the area made up for it by presenting the most peculiar ones. "Let me guess, the Yemens again?"

"No."

"Someone's trying to overthrow the Shah?"

"You've got it! Not bad for a Soviet Union expert."

"Who's out to get him this time, the Iraqis or the Iranian chapter of the UCLA alumni club?"

"We're not sure who's out to get him. There have been some vague hints made to the embassy in Tehran and to CIA to the effect that a coup may be brewing but that the Iranians can handle it themselves. We're supposed to keep hands off. The trouble is that the people giving the unasked-for advice might possibly be part of the coup. State and CIA are wondering what kind of signals we want to send back."

"Who's giving the advice? Have we got a line on what might be behind it?"

"It sounds like everything's probably on the up and up, but I'd feel happier if the message had come through government channels. The contact was the same person in both cases. He's a colonel in SAVAK, fellow named Colonel Ziya, Rahmatollah Ziya. CIA says they've known him for years. He's way up near the top. They figure he's absolutely loyal to the Shah. He's one of the old-timers who rose under the Shah's father. Distinguished himself during an assassination attempt against the Shah back in the fifties by gunning down the assassin."

"That's what CIA says. What do they know about him at State?"

"I was just on the phone to INR. They give him high marks too, but they also feel there may be a cleavage in SAVAK between the new boys and the old-timers, for what that's worth."

Holachek shook his blocky, crewcut head slowly. "Doesn't sound like much. The new boys are the ones who stage the coups; and when they do use a senior officer, they use him as a figurehead, not as a contact man. Anyway, doesn't the Shah have a super agency spying on SAVAK to put the fear in those guys in case they get any ideas?"

"Yeah, the Inspectorate, a handful of high-ranking true believers known only to the Shah."

"So, what's the problem? If your Colonel What's-his-name isn't kosher, the Shah should be able to find it out by himself."

"The Shah *should* be prepared to handle it. Still, State and

40

CIA are both looking for a little reassurance because there's another problem, too."

"What's that?"

"They're getting reports in about a rumor circulating in Iran concerning the reappearance of the Twelfth Imam."

The National Security Advisor ran his beefy hands despairingly through his short blond hair. "I knew it! If it's not the Arabs and Israelis pissing on each other, it's some weird sort of sideshow. All right, tell me who the Twelfth Imam is."

"It's not all that complicated," said Keller, grinning. "The first Imam was Ali ibn Abi-Talib; the second was Hasan ibn Ali; the third was Hossein ibn Ali; the fourth was . . ."

"Enough. A general outline will do just as well."

"Right, a general outline it is. You're missing some great stuff, though. The Iranians are Muslims, you got that?"

"I'm right with you."

"There's a Muslim belief that before the Last Judgment and the end of the world a kind of Messiah will come and rule the world in a millennium of peace and justice. This Messiah is called the Mahdi."

"That's the fellow who raised hell in the Sudan back in the nineteenth century, isn't it?"

"That's what he called himself. But a lot of people have called themselves the Mahdi in Middle Eastern history. It's the most common form of political revolt sanctioned by Islamic religion."

"But who's the Twelfth Imam?"

"He's the Iranian version of the Mahdi. The Iranians are Shiite Muslims. They believe that the true leader of all the Muslims is called the Imam. They count twelve Imams with the last one mysteriously disappearing in the ninth century. Since that time, they say he has been governing the world from concealment. He rules the world while in hiding the way the sun warms the earth when it is behind a cloud. Nice image, isn't it? Meaningless, but nice. Anyway, they believe that the Mahdi will not be some new Messiah but the Twelfth Imam, also called the

Hidden Imam, returned to usher in the end of the world."

"Very interesting. Remind me that I owe you an explanation of the differences between Russian Orthodox ritual and Greek Orthodox ritual."

Keller continued unperturbed. "The point is that half a dozen of the greatest revolutions in Middle Eastern history have started with people calling themselves the Mahdi or the Twelfth Imam. So if there's a rumor about a new Messiah at the same time we get told that there may be a coup brewing and that we should keep our hands out of it, it raises some obvious questions."

"All very dangerous if you make the assumption that the Iranian secret police are a bunch of religious cranks."

"Agreed. To get worried you would have to make that assumption."

"Anything more?"

"Nope, that's it."

"Fine. Tell State and CIA that our policy, as always, is one of non-interference in Iranian affairs."

Keller was already heading toward the door. "Unwilling to see a born-again Muslim come to power?" He shut the door behind him before he could hear any reply. In any case, he knew there would be none.

An hour later he was lunching on Szechuan fried pork and bean curd family-style in a small Chinese restaurant below street level on Avenue H not far from the State Department. With him was Frank Quintana, the Iranian specialist in INR, the department's Intelligence and Research Division. Professorially bespectacled and reserved looking, Bill Keller had leapfrogged in a prodigious manner up the academic ladder at a remarkably young age, while Keller's exact contemporary and one-time classmate in graduate school, Frank Quintana, had defied a dark romantic appearance that made him look like a secret agent to follow a more traditional bureaucratic route as a foreign service officer. The latter's present tour in INR made him far less important than Keller in the corridors of power, but their friendship had remained close, and Keller respected Quintana's expertise in Iranian matters in the same way that Quintana respected his in Arab-Israeli affairs.

"Holachek wasn't interested in all my lore about the Twelfth Imam, then?" Quintana asked his friend.

"I didn't think he would be. It had to be brought to his attention, though, in case anything develops down the road. Frankly, I don't think he was interested in your Colonel Ziya either. The office is full up right now with trying to play honest armsbroker for the Arabs and Israelis, and he really doesn't have time for the Shah to be overthrown."

"As long as it's in our files that the information was sent on up, it saves our hide if it actually happens."

"What do they think in the Near East Division?"

"They don't have time to think over there. I got a buzz from Milton Kaufman over at CIA, though. He's got a bee in his bonnet that the thing could be tied in with the Islamic Marxists."

"Are they out throwing bombs again?"

"No. That's why he thinks there could be a tie-in. There hasn't been a machinegunning, a bombing, a student strike, or a demonstration in favor of the return of the veil for over a month. No sign of infighting among the crazies, either. He thinks it's too quiet. There's also been some unusual running back and forth between Tehran, New York, and East Berlin by Iranian students they have their eye on as Islamic Marxists."

"How unusual?"

"Not very. The Soviet liners are known to keep pretty close contact with their exiled gurus in Berlin. It's just that the Islamic Marxists per se aren't usually seen making the trip."

"Islamic Marxism is a bunch of bullshit anyway, isn't it? That's the impression I get about the Arab variety."

Quintana emptied the last of the bean curd onto his plate. "Bullshit ideology never prevented anyone from trying a coup. You remember what Ben Groves used to say in lecture about Islamic Marxism?"

"Vaguely. I can't say I've retained very much from his course."

"It was his idea that the only thing preventing idealists seeking equality and brotherhood for all Muslims from becoming Marxists is that Marx's philosophy is atheistic. The utopia is the same: a world of perfect equality; but despite that, they appear to be inherently contradictory philosophies. He used to make the point that the same thing could be said, more or less, about the philosophies of Plato and Aristotle vis-à-vis Christianity. If the medieval Christian thinkers could baptize Plato and Aristotle for the convenience of utilizing their thought, modern Muslim thinkers should be capable of making Marx pray to Allah five times a day so that they can use his thought. You just have to look at it from a utilitarian standpoint."

"I can see why I got so little out of his course," said Keller, breaking open his fortune cookie and pulling out the tiny strip of paper. " 'You will receive wonderful news from a friend.' "

Quintana cracked open the other cookie. " 'You will soon make a long trip.' Christ, these things get duller and duller every year."

Two blocks from the restaurant they paused on the street corner where their paths separated.

"We'll have to get together and do this again when things are less hectic," said Frank with a parting handshake.

"Right. I'd like to talk about what you people expect to happen when the Shah finally goes down. Do you think his son will ever sit on the throne?"

"If he does, we'll set up an office pool on how many days he remains there. With luck, you'll draw a low number."

"As bad as that. Well, we'll have to talk about it sometime."

With that they parted, Quintana heading for the State Department and Keller for the Executive Office Building.

44

CHAPTER **6**

Ramadan in Nishapur was a bad time of year for dining out. The alternative, however, was to lunch at the Kamel residence, which was even worse. Mrs. Kamel was not unwilling to prepare a meal for their American guest, but no one in the family violated the obligatory daytime fast. Ben Groves did not object to eating alone in such a situation, but the first few times he ate at the Kamels' during Ramadan, Mr. Kamel felt obligated to sit and talk to him while he ate, eying the lunch hungrily the entire time. It was this that drove Groves to taking his lunches out.

He quickly discovered that he had only two choices. There was a modest hotel run by Armenian Christians that served food, but it was also the only place in town that served alcohol, and this gave it a bad reputation in the religiously conservative community. Under different circumstances, Groves would not have hesitated to take his lunches there, but since this trip was devoted to studying the cult of Hossein Makfuf, he did not wish to offend Muslim sensibilities unnecessarily.

The other possibility was a chelo kebab restaurant situated

near the main intersection where the long-distance buses traveling between Tehran and Mashhad made their Nishapur stop. Since travelers were religiously exempt from fasting during Ramadan, when a bus arrived for a short stop there would be a sudden rush of passengers gobbling down mounds of buttered chelo rice and strips of succulent broiled kebab, which the suffering waiters stoically served them.

Groves made a point of going to the restaurant when it was usually still empty around eleven o'clock so he could begin his meal in peace before the first midday bus arrived. Usually he ate slowly, reviewing his field notes and planning his afternoon's activities.

In the three weeks he had been in Nishapur he had discovered that change had taken place not only in the modern city but also in the ruins of the great medieval city some three kilometers to the east. The small, upright plaster niche which had held the tombstone of Hossein Makfuf when he had first discovered it was no longer visible. Instead, there was a square, domed building of baked brick about five meters on a side. The building was painted white, and from the low dome there protruded a wooden pole from which a triangular green pennant waved in the breeze, a typical rural shrine marked with the green emblem of the family of the Prophet.

It had taken time and a certain amount of cajolery and pious mendacity, but Groves had finally persuaded the diminutive, ebullient mulla who was custodian of the new shrine that, even though he was not a Muslim, he might be permitted to enter the building since he had been divinely guided in the discovery of the holy tombstone. Thus, he was eventually able to see once again the peculiar stone. Now set into the wall of the shrine itself. Groves felt that this change alone made it look more genuine than before, especially since the slight light that entered through the tiny unglazed apertures in the dome, even when supplemented by candles, was insufficient to reveal the sharp, unweathered quality of the carved inscription. Aside from the stone, the candles, and a number of small, locally produced Baluchi carpets covering the brick floor, the shrine was empty.

Further conversation with the talkative custodian after the visit had disclosed several things that caused Groves to modify his plan of research. Initially, he had intended to spend two months in Nishapur and then go to the great shrine cities of Qom and Mashhad to talk to the religious authorities about their reactions to the new cult. But the mulla custodian pointed out to him various places in the vicinity of the shrine where hungry workers were desultorily at work with shovels and baskets. This was the first step, he explained, in the preparation of giant prayer grounds for pilgrims. It was to be completed by the beginning of the month of Moharram, when the annual ten-day period of mourning for the martyred Third Imam would, for the first time, be celebrated by a pilgrimage to the shrine of Hossein Makfuf, the martyr's great-grandson. Fifty thousand pilgrims were expected for the holy occasion, and a great deal of preparation would be needed to accommodate them.

Groves privately doubted that the anticipated pilgrimage could turn out to be anything short of a disaster, given that the chaotic landscape of craggy ruins, pockmarked by the deep pits dug by treasure hunters and strewn with unidentifiable remnants of mud-brick walls and buildings, would have to be leveled to accommodate the mob, and neither the work force nor the four-month time period seemed adequate for the task. And this was not counting the logistical problems of providing food, water, and shelter for thousands of pilgrims.

Groves regretted that the religious movement he had set in motion was apparently going to result in the leveling and reuse of the central part of the ruins, thus making future archaeological work impossible. Still, the opportunity to study a major pilgrimage center at the moment of inception was not to be missed. Accordingly, he resolved to center his activities in Nishapur until the end of Moharram so that he could record every step in the development of the pilgrimage.

Groves settled into a daily routine of touring the planned

prayer grounds to monitor their construction, talking to residents of the city who might stand to profit from or be discommoded by a massive influx of pilgrims, and keeping track of the pilgrims who arrived in town and what they did after arrival. The latter activity, he realized, would become impossible as Moharram approached and the pilgrim traffic mushroomed, but he hoped that what he learned from and about the early arrivals would enable him to make worthwhile generalizations about the pilgrim throng as a whole.

Daily over his midday meal he studied the occupants of the buses from Tehran, which stopped in Nishapur every day at roughly the same time. Whenever Groves heard the strident blast of a vehicle's air horn blowing pedestrians, bicyclists, and sheep off the street as it roared into town, he put down his field notes and prepared to observe the disembarking passengers. Most of them eventually returned to the bus for the final leg of the trip into Mashhad, and the few who did not were most frequently met by family or gave other indications of being Nishapur natives. In time, however, the pilgrims would begin to come in larger numbers, and it was sensible to cultivate the habit of observing new arrivals.

It was by reason of this habitual observation that Groves happened one day to notice a young couple getting off a bus from Tehran. The man, appearing to be in his late twenties, was tall and slender. By his well-cut checked suit and Italianate shoes he was identifiable as a well-to-do city person, probably from Tehran.

It was his companion, however, who particularly attracted Groves's attention. She was of roughly the same age, slightly built, and draped in a chadur that effectively concealed her body and reduced her face to a mouth, nose, and two dark eyes set in a circle of blue paisley cloth. Strangely, for an Iranian woman, she did not seem to be able to manage her chadur very effectively. Artfully used, the drapery that served instead of the outlawed veil could be an elegant and even enticing garment, but in this case it seemed more like a hindrance, to the extent that at one point she pulled its lower portion aside entirely to extract something from her pocket. It was then that Groves noticed that she was wearing blue jeans. His eye caught on the tiny red label sticking from the seam of the rear pocket identifying the blue jeans as the product of Levi Strauss and Co.

Groves mulled over this peculiarity while the bus passengers clamored for food. A pair of genuine Levi's was a rare enough sight in the Iranian boondocks, but on a woman wearing a traditional chadur it was truly extraordinary. He regretted that the couple was obviously destined to continue on to Mashhad. But even as he was regretting this the bus's air horn blasted most of the diners out of their seats and caused them to rush to the cashier's desk and into the street for reboarding. However, the young couple calmly remained seated.

When the bus pulled away, they were still sitting at the rickety wooden table with the oilcloth cover. Aside from the small bags they had gotten off the bus with, they seemed to have no luggage. No one had appeared to meet them, and they did not give the impression that they were expecting anyone. Groves's curiosity was fully aroused to the point that with barely a second thought he arose to follow them when they left the restaurant. He supposed that they were a married couple from Tehran come to Nishapur to visit his or her relatives, but it would do no harm to see where they were actually going.

This initial supposition was upset by the elegant young man's very first action. He stopped another pedestrian and obviously asked directions, getting a long speech and a lot of pointing and hand waving in return. Since it was not really feasible to get lost in Nishapur, the interrogation clearly suggested that the couple had probably not been in town before.

Keeping a good distance to the rear, Groves followed the pair eastward down the main street. When they reached the traffic circle in front of Omar Khayyam High School they continued across it in an eastward direction. On the far side they stopped a second person to ask directions, and again the answer was an elaborate one. By now Groves was entirely confused as to where they could be going. The traffic circle had been built on the very edge of town thirty years before, but there were still only a few buildings and almost no residences along the tree-lined highway east of it. Nor did the highway they were starting down pass through another town for at least twenty kilometers. Only two possibilities remained. Either the couple was headed for one of the peasant villages off the road to the north or the south, which seemed out of the question given their sophisticated dress, or they were headed for the ruins of the medieval city.

Then Groves realized that there was only one realistic possibility: these two young people from Tehran could only be devotees of Hossein Makfuf and had come to visit the shrine of the blind saint.

CHAPTER 7

Jamshid Ansari and Zhaleh Hekmat were not unaware of the tall American shambling along behind them. Groves would stand out on any Iranian street, not so much for his unusual height, gangling frame, and light sandy hair, as for his crepe-soled Wallabees, Eisenhower-style gray windbreaker, and blue baseball cap perched precariously on the crown of his head. In addition, the young Iranians were particularly attuned to the possibility of being followed. It pleased them that the American tourist was the only person who had noticed their arrival and that *he* had given up following them a short distance past the traffic circle.

"He's stopped," murmured Zhaleh after a surreptitious glance over her shoulder.

"Good," said her companion. "He could hardly be a SAVAK agent, in any case, and it's not likely that the CIA thinks we're important enough to track down way out here."

Two kilometers past the Omar Khayyam traffic circle a wide paved road turned off sharply to the south. After several hundred meters the road climbed over the embankment of the railroad track and dead-ended in front of two enclosed gardens. Behind the wall of one rose the beautiful turquoise dome of a shrine dedicated to Mohammad Mahruq, an obscure medieval saint. More easily seen through the modern steel fence of the other were the tall, parabolic arches of the recently constructed concrete and tile monument to Nishapur's famous poet Omar Khayyam. The tree-studded gardens surrounding the shrine and the monument made the area a favorite picnicking spot in the otherwise treeless Nishapur plain, and the two sites also constituted the city's only recognized tourist attraction.

Jamshid and Zhaleh did not follow the road to its end, however. Just before the crossing of the railroad track they turned off on a dirt road heading east, into the heart of the medieval ruins on the outskirts of which the shrine and the monument were located. They walked for only a hundred meters or so down the side road and then stopped. A cool autumn breeze at their backs swirled in front of them the dust kicked up by their footsteps. In the distance, between the remains of the old walls of the inner city still standing some four meters high and the arrow-straight gash of the railroad track, they spotted a small white building with a green pennant flying from the roof.

"That must be it," said Jamshid. "The place of two miracles: the miracle of the discovery of the tomb of Hossein Makfuf and the miracle of the return of the Hidden Imam." He emitted a soft laugh, which was rewarded by a sardonic look from the girl. Then they turned around and retraced their steps to the paved road. This time they continued down the road, following it between the fence of the Omar Khayyam garden and the motel-like guesthouse built on the opposite side of the pavement for official guests of the Shah. They finally turned in at the gate in the garden wall surrounding the large and stately shrine mosque of Mohammad Mahruq. Under the soaring mosaic-covered archway leading into the shrine a young mulla accosted them; after a brief exchange of words, he led them into the deeply shadowed interior.

They emerged into the sun again with blinding suddenness on a second-floor arcade and then returned to semi-darkness on being shown into a featureless brick room sparsely furnished as an office with a plain wooden desk and a scattering of metal folding chairs. Jamshid was greeted by a senior mulla with a scraggly salt-and-pepper beard and unexpected light-blue eyes and by a short unshaven man in a navy-blue business suit who introduced himself as Chief of Education Ebrahim Borumand. The presence of Zhaleh Hekmat was an immediate bone of contention.

"Who is this woman?" demanded the mulla peremptorily.

"She is my associate, Zhaleh Hekmat. She will stay here in Nishapur to manage our business at this end."

"That is impossible!" The mulla swirled his brown robe around him and sat himself behind the desk. "Ayatollah Pirzadeh did not say that your agent would be a woman. We cannot have a woman here."

"Ayatollah Pirzadeh did not know," replied Jamshid evenly. "I told him only that I would assign the task to a member of the central committee of the Muslim Marxist Alliance. Zhaleh is on the central committee."

At this point the Chief of Education intervened with the placating voice of an experienced administrator. "I am sure you will appreciate, Mr. Ansari and Miss Hekmat, that nothing personal is intended. It is simply that the job to be done is not proper work for a woman. If we fail, we shall all certainly be killed. We must have strong people who can face this fact."

"Mr. Borumand," said Zhaleh softly, speaking for the first time, "you should not judge what you do not know. If you are concerned about my intellectual abilities, I have a degree in electrical engineering from an American university. If it's my courage and revolutionary zeal that concern you, I can tell you that it was I who placed the bomb that killed the American air force attaché last year. But I suspect that as a bureaucrat you may actually be concerned about something else. On that matter, if you give a thought to my family name, you will realize that both my father and my uncle are members of the Imperial Senate by appointment of the Shah."

The Chief of Education looked taken aback. Behind his swarthy visage Jamshid and Zhaleh knew he was calculating the likelihood of senatorial pressure destroying his career. Pirzadeh had warned Jamshid that Borumand could not be relied upon. He had been recruited into the plot out of the necessity of controlling matters in Nishapur and by means of promises that Pirzadeh had no intention of honoring. Personal advancement was his sole motivation. If his services became unnecessary, Pirzadeh had indicated that they could be dispensed with, permanently.

The light of decision finally lit in the chief's eyes, and he went over to speak into the mulla's ear. The man of religion shook his white turban vehemently in disagreement.

"While you are considering the matter," interrupted Jamshid in a civil tone, "I would like to point out four advantages in having Zhaleh here instead of a man. First, she will not be conspicuous here in Nishapur in the way other members of our central committee would be. Second, no one will speak to her and ask her questions as they would do with a man. Third, her chadur will serve to keep her appearance concealed."

"Does she wear the chadur when she is in Tehran?" asked the mulla with caustic skepticism.

"Always. All of the women in the Muslim Marxist Alliance wear the chadur. It is a sign of the difference between men and women, and it is ordained by the Holy Qoran." The mulla was visibly mollified, and for the first time since they had entered the room cast a look upon the modestly shrouded Zhaleh. "As to the fourth advantage of having a woman here, it is a condition of our cooperation in the revolution. At this stage I do not believe it will be possible for you to overthrow the Shah without our cooperation."

"Where will the woman stay?" said the mulla in a sullen but accommodating voice.

"We thought she would stay here at the shrine. You certainly have women to do cooking and cleaning. She can be here in the guise of a servant, but, of course, she must have a separate room."

"It will be done," said the mulla tersely as he fingered his straggly beard. "What now of the Twelfth Imam? Have you word of him?"

"Yes. All is going well. Ayatollah Pirzadeh says that he has arrived at Qom and will remain there for several weeks. That is all he would tell me. But I am supposed to report to him on the preparations being made here."

"We have sent reports regularly," protested Borumand.

"That is true, but the Ayatollah desires corroboration. You must take us out to the shrine and show us."

The mulla rose abruptly and strode to the door. "Come." The others followed him out into the sunshine, Zhaleh Hekmat modestly trailing at the end of the line of men.

It was less than a kilometer from the magnificent shrine of Mohammad Mahruq to the rudimentary one of Hossein Makfuf, but the way was uneven and covered with a litter of bricks and scattered hummocks of rubble. It took them a considerable time to make their way. As they finally drew near, they saw the unmistakable figure of Ben Groves just coming out of the small white shrine with the much shorter mulla custodian behind him. The four stopped in their tracks, but there was no way to conceal their destination.

Groves too stopped and looked at the senior mulla, the Chief of Education, and the easily recognizable young couple from the bus. He waited for them to come closer. Then he realized that they were obviously waiting for him to depart, and he hurriedly mounted his bicycle and pedaled off down the newly cleared path that linked the humble shrine to the main dirt road. It annoyed him to be forced to retreat, since his purpose in returning to town and fetching his bicycle had been to follow the couple from the bus and speak to them. More than ever he wondered who they were to warrant the company of high officials in visiting the Hossein Makfuf shrine.

He determined to bend every effort to find out.

Once the professor had disappeared from view, the party of four continued on toward the shrine, but Groves's unexpected appearance had distracted them.

"Who is that man?" Zhaleh asked. "He followed us to the edge of town after we got off the bus."

"He's Professor Benjamin Groves, an American," Borumand replied. "You may have seen his name. He discovered the tomb of Hossein Makfuf many years ago, and now it seems he has returned to study the shrine and the pilgrims who come to it. Of course, since the shrine has not been officially recognized by the Ministry of Culture and Art, I am not directly sponsoring or supporting his work. But unofficially I have welcomed him and assisted him in finding a place to stay. He is harmless, I am sure."

"Still, it would be better if he were not here," said Jamshid. "How long is he planning to remain in Nishapur?"

"Until the end of Moharram, I believe."

"Just long enough. Can he be sent away?"

The Chief of Education threw out his hands in a sign of hopelessness. "For what reason? He has letters from the ministry permitting him to carry out his study. It would be very suspicious to order him to leave. Besides, it is not necessary. He is not a political man; he will not cause difficulties."

"He's right, Jamshid," said Zhaleh. "We will simply have to tolerate his presence. Anything else might attract attention."

The next day Ben Groves was once again consuming an impious plate of chelo kebab in the restaurant next to the bus stop. As usual, there was a rush of passengers every time a bus arrived or departed. It did not escape his notice, however, when Jamshid Ansari appeared at the last possible moment to board a bus heading for Tehran. Nor did it escape his notice that this time the young man was traveling alone.

CHAPTER **8**

Ambassador Ralston Dermott was not pleased with the message that the morning's cable traffic had brought him. It was Freddy Desuze's misfortune that there was no one else upon whom Dermott could vent his displeasure. Desuze was sitting in a black captain's chair with a gold Princeton seal on the back while the agitated ambassador paced around him.

"I disapprove of this completely, Desuze. I'm going to send a cable to the secretary making my complaint official. You CIA boys have got to get it into your heads that you can't continue playing cloak and dagger the way you used to during the Cold War. Just because you saved the Shah's throne back in fifty-three doesn't mean you have to poke your nose into every two-bit conspiracy." Much of Freddy Desuze's success as a covert employee of the CIA was a product of the bland, mindless expression that settled so easily over his porcine features. "Do you realize," the ambassador complained, "that I've been in Tehran less than a month? This sort of thing could kill my tour. I don't see why we can't inform somebody in the Iranian government about what we're doing. Someone must be loyal. Who's Kaufman, anyway?"

"Milton Kaufman, Mr. Ambassador, first-rate analyst, fifteen years with the agency, follows Iran like a hawk. If he says there's a threat, he's probably right."

"But why can't the Iranians handle it? We surely have contacts in Iranian intelligence. Why can't we just tell them what we know and let them run with it? No chance of someone getting upset if they find out we're skulking around behind their backs."

"You'll notice in the cable, sir, that Kaufman thinks SAVAK, or elements within SAVAK, may be involved. Giving information to SAVAK might be delivering it to the wrong side. He also says that Emmanuel Holachek wants it to appear that we're keeping out of it."

The gray-haired diplomat continued to stalk around the room. Suddenly he stopped and stared at Desuze. "Do *you* believe it? A conspiracy of Islamic clergy, Islamic Marxists, and SAVAK? Does that make sense to you? Does it? It does not." He snapped his eyes away and gazed through the window at the carefully watered and manicured lawns of the embassy compound.

"If you'll pardon me for saying so, sir," said Desuze with his slight drawl, "Kaufman's theory is not entirely unbelievable." The ambassador turned and glared at the fat middle-aged spy. "I don't know how much you know about this country, sir, but in the last century and the early part of this one the Islamic clergy were both revolutionary and militantly against the Shah when they thought he wasn't doing right by the country. One time he sold the rights for a tobacco monopoly to a foreign company, and the mullas announced a ban on smoking tobacco. And you know what? Everyone stopped smoking tobacco. The Shah had to cancel the monopoly. It takes a lot of power to do that, sir. Can you imagine the National Council of Churches banning tobacco in the U.S. and having everyone obey them?"

"That's ancient history, Desuze."

Freddy drawled on as if there had been no interruption. "And then the part about the Islamic Marxists. Well, the intellectuals played ball with the clergy back at the time of the Constitutional Revolution of 1906, and there's no reason to suppose they couldn't get together again. These student Marxists fancy themselves intellectuals. Some of them were hand-in-glove with a few radical mullas back in the fifties and sixties."

"And SAVAK?"

"Yup, that's the tough one. Per capita output in that outfit is pretty damn low, but SAVAK's so big that they have a finger on just about everything that's happening. If I had to guess, I'd put them down as provocateurs trying to smoke out the radicals, but apparently the information people get back in D.C. makes them think it's something more serious. And another thing, Mr. Ambassador, if I may change the subject, if the Shah does get put down by this thing, whatever it is, I don't think you would want to be thought to have hindered our gathering information about it."

"I never realized the agency gave lessons in soothing the feelings of diplomats. Obviously I don't want the Shah overthrown while I'm ambassador; but, goddamn it, I don't want a spying scandal either. If Briggs over in Saudi Arabia can say he wants Saudi-American relations to be as close as Canadian-American relations, I can say I want Iranian-American relations to be as close as Anglo-American relations. I'm not against investigating a projected coup; I just think we shouldn't do it behind the Iranians' backs."

"It's for their own good, sir. Besides, I have my orders to carry out, and I'll have to stick to them until I hear otherwise."

The ambassador's jowly face sagged dispiritedly. "What exactly are your plans?"

"I guess I haven't made any yet. Cable just came this morning. I suppose I'll see a few people and ask some questions. If there's something big enough to be serious, someone's got to know about it."

At midnight Freddy Desuze and Susan Bengston were sitting beside the bandstand in the basement nightclub of a somewhat seedy establishment known as The German Hotel. It being Ramadan, the single dimly lit room was packed with raucous people who had restrained their appetites throughout the daylight hours in order to satisfy them after dark. The sight of people who had fasted like good Muslims during the day pouring down forbidden liquor like godless infidels at night suggested a moral lesson, but it was the obscurity of the rendezvous that had attracted the pair of Americans rather than a desire to savor the hypocrisy of Tehran society.

Susan Bengston's long blond hair turned alternately red, purple, and blue under the rotating lights bathing the tiny bandstand, where a four-piece combo was trying to sound like a fifteen-piece disco orchestra.

"How's your boyfriend treating you, Suzy?" This would not be the first time that Freddy Desuze had drawn information from the bedroom of the Minister of Culture and Art, nor the first time in her government career that Susan Bengston had traded discretion for a good mark in the books of the CIA.

"Okay. He seems pretty busy these days."

"Anything special?"

"What kind of special?"

"I don't know. Unusual. Particularly in the religious area."

"Well, he has his radio broadcasts. He gets tense about those sometimes."

"Not unusual enough."

The well-proportioned young woman played with the swizzle stick in her vodka lime and gazed about the room, trying to focus her thoughts as the shadows of dancing bodies distracted her eyes.

"The other day he was talking about the Hossein Makfuf cult," she said tentatively.

"What's that?"

"I don't know." Her momentarily purple profile accompanied the words with a shrug. "I gather it's some sort of lower-class religious cult centered on that tomb Professor Groves discovered out in Nishapur."

"I remember Groves," said Freddy brightly. "He kept me company on that trip I had to take out to Mashhad. Had a good time. I talked his ear off. I remember now him saying he was studying some sort of tomb."

"Don't ask me for the details," replied the blonde. "It all sounded very obscure when he explained it to me."

"What's Hormozi's involvement in it?"

"I don't know exactly, but I gather that as Minister of Culture and Art it's up to him to make an official determination about whether the tombstone is real or not."

"And, if he says it's not, this Hossein Makfuf cult is going to be pissed off, right?"

"I suppose. But somehow I think there's more to it than that. I recall him saying that it was very ticklish having the Shah wanting you to do one thing and the Shah's bodyguard wanting you to do the opposite. I think that was in reference to the Hossein Makfuf matter."

Freddy Desuze was suddenly paying very close attention. "Did he say bodyguard, or SAVAK?"

"I've never heard him utter the word SAVAK, even in his sleep."

"But *bodyguard* could be a euphemism for SAVAK."

"Possibly. I sometimes think he's deliberately cautious in what he says to me."

"In other words, this Hossein Makfuf character might be someone that the Shah and SAVAK disagree on."

"Isn't that going a little far? SAVAK can't disagree with the Shah, can it? I just thought he was talking about one of these things where the President wants to ride in a convertible and the Secret Service wants him to use an armored car."

"But you said it was in connection with Hossein Makfuf."

"I think so. I can't remember exactly. I don't take notes, you know."

"You know what I'm going to do, Suzy? I'm going to mention

you in my report. You're a good little agent. You wouldn't like to top it off by telling me that the handsome Dr. Hormozi is conspiring to overturn the government, would you?"

"Why should I? If he succeeded, I might become an empress. The most I'll get from having nice things said about me in Washington is a quicker promotion to GS-14, and with the current inflation rate even that doesn't mean much." After a second she added, "That doesn't mean I won't take it, though."

Later that night, after dropping a tipsy Susan Bengston off at her home in the respectable suburb of Daudiyeh, Freddy Desuze placed a phone call to Jamshid Ansari. An unlikely association between the two men had been formed during political infighting among the Iranian student left. Freddy knew that Jamshid would be utterly silent on the activities of his own Muslim Marxist Alliance, but if a rival organization was involved, he might find it useful to blow the whistle on them. Desuze and Ansari fixed upon a meeting in the park at the foot of the Shahyad monument.

CHAPTER 9

Massive yet exquisitely curved, the Shahyad monument bestrode the western entrance to Tehran like a giant resplendently uniformed eunuch standing guard in the royal palace, informing by his majestic presence all who approached that they were on the threshold of the court of the King of Kings, the Light of the Aryans, the Shah of Iran. Shaped like the lower third of a truncated Eiffel Tower, but with the infinitely more delicate lines permitted by its poured-concrete construction, the monument was intended as an eternal emblem of the Iranian monarchy. With foresight it had been placed on the western edge of the city to impress foreign visitors coming into the capital from Mehrabad Airport.

Beyond the monument to the northwest, on land that had previously been unwatered waste, was a giant complex of half-completed high-rise buildings, a city in itself that would eventually house tens of thousands of the capital's burgeoning population. Around the double base of the monument, the interior of an immense traffic circle had been transformed into a luxuriant park with lawns and formal flower beds separated by a radiating network of paths providing access to the monument's museum and observation deck.

At nine in the morning Jamshid Ansari found the corpulent Freddy Desuze waiting for him on a bench in the southeast quadrant of the park. Freddy had chosen the southeast to get the best of the morning sun's warmth on a crisp late-fall day. The haze of exhaust fumes from the morning rush hour was unusually light because people were going late and lethargically to work during Ramadan.

Freddy was in no particular rush to get down to business since he was still uncertain as to what he was looking for. They discussed the weather, Jamshid's wardrobe, student activities at the university where Jamshid taught, and Iran's chances in the World Cup. If Freddy was prepared to delay putting direct questions, Jamshid was equally prepared to postpone refusing to answer them, so it was almost an hour before Freddy moved to a more pertinent topic.

"Would you happen to know a Colonel Rahmatollah Ziya, Jamshid?"

"No." Jamshid was happy to be able to start off with a truthful answer.

"Would you have any idea why I'm asking you if you know him?"

"No." Almost truthful.

"Things have been very quiet lately on campus. Any particular reason?" Jamshid's expression was negative. "You haven't stopped quarreling with the Maoists and the Stalinists, have you?"

"We seem to be getting along somewhat better."

"Mm-hmmm. All quiet and peaceful, then. Nothing happening."

"The students are very studious this year."

"Well, good to hear it. There was something else. What was it? Oh, yes. Would you happen to know anything at all about the rumors going around concerning the Twelfth Imam? You know, about his coming back to earth?"

"Not a thing." As he uttered the words, Jamshid visibly froze, his eyes fixed at a point beyond Freddy's shoulder. Casually the fat American glanced behind him. The only person in sight was a brown-robed mulla with a closely trimmed black beard and heavy black-rimmed glasses pacing slowly between two beds of end-of-the-season flowers while fingering his string of amber prayer beads. Freddy slowly turned back to face Jamshid.

"Well, I'm glad everything's going so well. It looks like a peaceful season. If you should hear anything interesting about Colonel Ziya, you might let me know, though. Would you do that?" Jamshid gave a stiff nod. "That's good. I'd better be pushing along, then. It was nice of you to meet me here." The fat man lifted himself heavily from the bench and brushed off his trousers. "Are we heading the same way? I could give you a lift."

Jamshid hesitated and then shook his head. "I have my own car. It's parked over on the airport road."

Freddy nodded. "Okay. Nice seeing you." He gave a parting wave as he moved slowly off down the path.

Jamshid had stood up to say goodbye. Now, white-faced, he sat down again on the bench as he watched two husky young working-class types turn onto the pathway behind the American. From the distance he could not be certain, but he felt reasonably sure that he had seen the two before in the inner room of the zurkhaneh in Arak. Two others unobtrusively moved into place at the end of the path where it intersected the sidewalk running around the circumference of the traffic circle.

Two-thirds of the way to the highway the American suddenly broke out running at a right angle to the pathway. His speed for a man of his weight was impressive, and the four pursuers, caught by surprise, had a lot of ground to make up. That the athletic young Iranians would quickly be able to overtake the American's lead was not in doubt, but it was obvious that

Freddy hoped to make it to the traffic-filled highway before they did. With luck, he could use the traffic as a shield; directly opposite the point he was heading for was a possible refuge in the maze of scaffolding and excavation marking the edge of the West Tehran development project.

Jamshid's heart was racing; then it gave a lurch as two more Iranians leaped out of a parked car directly into Freddy's path. The heavy man was unable to stop. He ran directly into their arms, and in moments he had been rendered unconscious and dragged into the small Iranian-built Fiat, which quickly pulled away from the curb. As it made its way around the circle, Freddy's own blue Ford van pulled into the traffic behind it. It was only then that Jamshid realized that he was no longer alone on the bench. Ayatollah Pirzadeh was sitting quietly beside him fingering his amber beads.

"Very regrettable," he murmured. "But I told you we cannot allow our plans to be discovered. You said that your own security was satisfactory. It was a shock to find that you yourself were dealing with an agent of the CIA."

"But I wasn't," Jamshid stammered. "I told him nothing. Your instructions were to act in our normal manner insofar as possible. If I had refused to see him, he would have been suspicious. In the past I have agreed to see him because the Americans have been able to help us control our enemies among Iranian students in the U.S. But this time I told him nothing." His mouth was dry.

"What did he want to know?"

"He asked about a colonel named Rahmatollah Ziya. I told him I didn't know who he was. That was all. I think he was just fishing for information without knowing what he was looking for. He also asked about the rumors of the Twelfth Imam's return. I told him I didn't know anything. I swear on the Qoran that's all that was said."

"You're worried, Jamshid," said the dark-visaged mulla in a mildly surprised tone of voice. "Surely you don't think I mistrust you personally. I was only acting to assist your own security measures. In fact, we're very pleased with what you have done. Sending Zhaleh Hekmat to Nishapur was a very sound idea, even though my colleagues at the shrine of Mohammad Mahruq heartily disapprove. From what you have reported and we have observed, your contacts with the Soviets have been quite successful as well. I understand the materials we require will arrive next month. There should be no difficulty in having them in place before Moharram."

"You haven't told me who will be in charge of that part of the plan, my people or yours."

"It will be up to your people to get the materials to Nishapur. We will take care of the installation."

"In other words, I am not to know what precisely they are to be used for."

"That is correct."

"And the Twelfth Imam?"

"A fine, inspiring man."

"Then you have met him personally?"

"I have been graced by his presence."

Jamshid was regaining his composure. "Tell me, am I to be so graced, as well?"

"Unfortunately, not until his miraculous revelation when the entire world shall see him and know that he has returned."

"For reasons of security."

"For reasons of security. When the fat American's friends come to ask questions about his disappearance, it will be better that you do not have too many answers."

"I swear to you I will tell no one anything."

"And I will do my best to help you keep your oath. You may be interested to know how I found out about your meeting here today in time to take action. Your telephone is tapped by SAVAK, and what SAVAK knows we know. It also stands to reason that what SAVAK knows the CIA may know as well. In other words, I think it is possible that more American agents will come to see you once the fat one's body is found."

"Then you are going to kill him?"

67

The dark eyes behind the glasses popped open in surprise. "But of course. He surely must be dead by now. But he is only a Christian. He will be driven up the Ab-i Ali road and rolled off one of the cliffs in his car. Everyone knows how dangerous that road is and how reckless we Iranians are as drivers. If God wills, his death will be taken as an accident."

Jamshid envisioned the barren crags of the Elburz Mountains and the tremendous canyons along the sides of which the Ab-i Ali road wound its tortuous way to Tehran from the Caspian Sea. Many a time on trips to the tropical beaches of the sea he had known drivers to pull over to the side of the road to look at the spectacular remains of an unfortunate truck or bus strewn in pieces on the canyon floor.

Shawwal:
The Third Month

CHAPTER **10**

In National Security Advisor Emmanuel Holachek's White House office an unscheduled meeting was taking place. The off-the-record gathering had begun in Bill Keller's office in the Executive Office Building and had crossed the street after a phone call to Holachek excited his interest. Attending the meeting besides Holachek and Keller, his assistant for Middle Eastern affairs, were Milton Kaufman, the balding fiftyish senior analyst who managed the Iranian desk at the CIA, and the wavy-haired, Hispanic-looking Frank Quintana, some fifteen years his junior and his opposite number in the State Department's Intelligence and Research Division.

Holachek was in the brusque, businesslike mood he affected when dealing with other departments. He reserved his relaxed, bantering manner for his own staff. The two styles together, when exposed to the press, created the desirable public image of a complicated personality capable of dealing with any variety of international crisis.

"Could you briefly go over with me, Milton, what you were

telling Bill in his office. Just enough to put me in the picture."

Kaufman was too experienced in the ways of powerful officials to be cowed by a stern voice. "You'll actually need a number of details, Mr. Holachek, to understand the situation. The Agency just this morning got word that the body of one of our people in Iran has been recovered and positively identified. He had been missing for two weeks. His name is Frederick Desuze; been on station as economics attaché with the embassy in Tehran for three years. Prior to that, an excellent record in Vietnam and Cambodia."

"In other words, a competent, experienced agent." Holachek's eyes narrowed to slits when he concentrated.

"Correct. He was found in his car at the bottom of a gorge about thirty miles from Tehran. Tire tracks leading off the road, no safety rail, skid marks of a second car, everything to indicate that someone came around a hairpin turn in the wrong lane and sideswiped him. Standard driving procedure in Iran; I've seen it almost happen myself."

"But this wasn't an accident?"

"It doesn't look like it. We lifted the whole wreck out with a helicopter. Hell of a job. The body was all banged up so it's not impossible that he died in the crash. There wasn't anything we could identify as indicating collision with another vehicle, but he could conceivably have swerved off the road or lost control without actually colliding with the other car. What makes it definite that he was dropped over the edge on purpose is that his radio is missing."

"Not in his apartment or office?"

"No, but it wouldn't be anyway. He made a big deal about being a radio nut, but the portable short-wave outfit he carried in his car actually had a concealed broadcast capacity built into it, complete with a scrambler circuit. It was used to keep in touch with him when he was out of Tehran. Whoever took the radio probably doesn't know what he's got, but Freddy certainly wouldn't have taken it out of the car deliberately."

"Was anything else missing?"

"Nope."

"So the agency thinks someone killed him. Why does that make it a matter for this office?"

"As far as we can tell, Mr. Holachek, Freddy Desuze was last seen alive the evening after he received an assignment from Washington to look into the possibility that a coup is brewing against the Shah. He had a few drinks with a woman in the International Communications Agency whom we've used from time to time to get information. That was about midnight. According to the woman—name of Susan Bengston—Desuze was interested in finding out if there was any unusual activity in the Ministry of Culture and Art. She's the minister's current girlfriend. Apparently he's a real fast climber in the government and has a taste for foreign blondes. From her report, it sounds like Freddy was getting right to work. The analysis we sent him singled out the Islamic Marxist underground, the upper ranks of the Muslim clergy, and some faction within SAVAK as possibly having a hand in the plans for a coup. The first two are groups this Hormozi, who's Minister of Culture and Art, could be expected to be in touch with. Apparently Susan Bengston didn't have anything to tell Desuze except that the minister was disturbed about some sort of decision he had to make concerning the authentication of an ancient tomb. She said Freddy jumped on it as something the Shah and SAVAK were in disagreement on, but her own opinion was that he was chasing a red herring."

Holachek held up his hand to stop the narrative. "What we have, then, is a dead agent, probably murdered, who disappeared just as he began investigating this possible coup. I presume you don't know what steps he was planning to take in this investigation."

Kaufman shook his head. "Ambassador Dermott had asked him exactly that earlier in the day and had not got an answer. Freddy was still trying to get a feel for the situation. Of course, we know the names of a lot of contacts he's used in the past, but we don't know which ones he might have been planning to see this time."

"Am I also correct," continued Holachek, "in assuming that the agency takes his death as evidence that a coup is definitely in the works?"

"Not the agency, Mr. Holachek. That's my own opinion. The agency doesn't think there's enough evidence."

"How cautious." Holachek swiveled his desk chair from facing the CIA analyst to facing Frank Quintana. "Now then, Mr. Quintana, what do you have to contribute?" The stern slitted eyes bored in.

Quintana had never before spoken directly with the National Security Advisor. "I concur with Mr. Kaufman's feeling that a coup could be in the making. This came up a month ago, and I didn't see it fitting together; but now I think it's a real possibility. Furthermore, I think Mr. Desuze may have been right in picking up the business about a medieval tombstone. This tombstone is of a blind holy man who died about twelve hundred years ago. It turned up several years back, and there's no way to tell for sure whether it's real or fake. The Ministry of Culture and Art is expected to make a proclamation on the subject. But, in the meantime, a kind of grassroots religious cult has grown up around this holy man. It's been snowballing very quickly in the last several months. There may be as many as twenty or thirty thousand pilgrims coming to pray at his tomb at the beginning of the month of Moharram."

"When's that?"

"Hmmm. Just about four months from now. It corresponds with early March in our calendar this year. Their religious year is shorter than ours, you know."

"Go on about the pilgrimage."

"Well, nothing about the pilgrimage except that it's supposed to be a big climax of this movement. The tie-in comes with some other reports we've got within the last few months predicting the return of the Twelfth Imam. He's a kind of Messiah figure."

"Yes, I know all about it," said Holachek authoritatively.

"The reason this is a tie-in is because the Twelfth Imam, who is supposed to return and bring in the millennium of peace and justice, is a relative of the man who's supposed to be buried in this tomb. A few days ago we got the first report of a rumor saying that the Twelfth Imam and the man in the tomb are the same person. They're not supposed to be, historically speaking, but this cult seems to be making up its own history. In other words . . ."

Holachek was leaning forward on his desk in full interest. "In other words, the Twelfth Imam could reappear at the time of the big pilgrimage and that could be the beginning of the coup."

"Exactly, Sir."

Holachek turned abruptly back to Kaufman. "Is that what you think too?"

"I think it's a definite possibility. There are some things that don't fit, like the SAVAK tie-in, but a religiously based coup would fit for either the conservative clergy who don't like the Shah or for the Islamic Marxist radicals."

"And how serious do you think it could be?"

"If it's well handled, it could be a real threat. Religious feeling cuts across all other loyalties in Iran. Some government people are good Muslims; others would be classed as sinners and hypocrites by any religion. The same goes for SAVAK, the military, probably even the Shah's personal bodyguard. Any of these groups might be affected by religious propaganda. Besides that, if the thing climaxes in front of tens of thousands of pilgrims, the Shah would have to think twice before ordering in the army. The soldiers might refuse to shoot and join the other side. And, to top it off, every year the first ten days of the month of Moharram are a period of ritual mourning all over Iran for a martyred saint who was related to the holy man Frank was just mentioning. In every city there are huge mobs in the street, processions, mass meetings in the mosques, intense religious feeling, and so forth. If the Shah took action against a popular religious figure at that particular moment, all hell could break loose."

"I begin to get the picture," said Holachek slowly. "So the Shah may not be able to trust even his own secret police."

"Not all of them, at least. And he probably couldn't tell in advance who would prove loyal and who wouldn't."

"I don't suppose we know who the Twelfth Imam is going to be or who's running the show—assuming there is a show being planned."

"No idea," said Quintana and Kaufman in unison. "That was what we were hoping to find out from Freddy Desuze," added Kaufman.

"Have you put someone else on it?"

"No, Sir," said Kaufman.

Holachek glared at him as if he had uttered a personal insult, but before he could reply Bill Keller intervened for the first time.

"Let me explain, Emmanuel. That's why Milton and Frank have come to us. CIA has a ten-man station in Tehran. But without exception they are known to the Iranian government. Some of them have regular contacts with SAVAK or the Iranian army; others are working under covers. None of them is really secret, however."

"So send in someone new."

"We don't have anyone to send, Mr. Holachek," said Kaufman.

Keller added. "The trouble is that everyone who knows Iran well enough to go in and do the job is already known to the Iranians. They're all people who've been stationed there before. If Freddy Desuze was killed because he was known to be an agent, which is a pretty likely possibility, the same thing could happen again. We can't trust SAVAK to be on our side—or on the Shah's."

"You're about to suggest something," Holachek said.

"That's right," said Keller. "The idea is to send in Frank Quintana instead of someone from the agency. Frank knows Iran; he knows everything we know about the coup; and he could be rotated into a regular embassy slot without suspicion because the Iranians know him to be an ordinary foreign service officer."

"And he's untrained," added Holachek.

"We could give him a crash course," said Kaufman.

"It's still a bad idea. But why does it come to me, anyway?" Keller replied. "Three reasons: the Assistant Secretary of State for Near Eastern Affairs flatly says no; Bennett at CIA won't have anything to do with it; and Ambassador Dermott in Tehran thinks Desuze died in a car accident and that the investigation should be dropped. That makes you the only one who can change their minds."

"And I think it's a bad idea."

"Yes, that's what you said," continued his assistant, "but you've given the go-ahead to a lot of bad ideas in the last three years."

Holachek grinned. "Name ten." Suddenly stern again he said, "I'll have to look into it further. It may be a bad idea, but it may be better than letting the Shah go down the tubes. I assume you're willing to do this, Mr. Quintana."

Frank Quintana nodded.

CHAPTER 11

Dr. Mohammad Hormozi left the low modern brick-and-glass edifice of the Iran-America Society in north Tehran after a rare, but not entirely unprecedented, mid-afternoon get-together in the private office of the society's charming program director. He felt remarkably satisfied and was confident that Miss Bengston did too. His Mercedes was parked in the crosswalk at the entrance to the society's courtyard. The driver was diligently wiping dust from the automobile's pearl-gray roof with a rag soaked in the jube. Today was the day in the weekly cycle for the deep concrete gutters in this part of Tehran to be flushed out, and the stream gurgling down the jube caused Hormozi to step carefully to keep his light-gray pin-striped trousers clean. It was this preoccupation that prevented him from noticing until he opened the door that someone was already sitting in the front seat.

"What are you doing here?" he said brusquely to his hawk-nosed private secretary Abbas Azad.

"I had to find you, Your Excellency," replied the young man with apologetic deference.

"You could have waited outside the car."

"I am sorry, Your Excellency. All the taxis were full, and the bus stops at the bottom of the hill. I tired myself hurrying to get here."

Slightly mollified, the Minister of Culture and Art slid into the back seat. "If it's so important, come back here with me." While the secretary shifted to the back seat, Hormozi raised the electrically operated window that sealed the passenger compartment off from the ears of the driver.

"I came to tell you that there is someone waiting for you at your office," said the secretary as soon as the car was underway.

"You could have telephoned me," said Hormozi. The young man stared modestly at the floor. "No, I suppose it's better you didn't. Tell me who's waiting for me."

"His name is Jamshid Ansari."

"The name is familiar."

"You have seen it. He is an instructor in architecture at the university. He did his graduate work in the United States on fellowships from the ministry."

"Of course, now I remember. He's from Rasht, I believe. His family owns the Golbahar tea company. I don't believe I've met him, though."

"Only at a reception for returning students, I think."

"Well, what's his business? Why did you let him wait at the office? He could have come back tomorrow."

"He won't state his business, Your Excellency. The reason I let him wait is because of the report on your desk, the one you asked me to compile on the Twelfth Imam."

"I've only had time to glance at it. What does it say?" The minister was distracted by the sight of two Scandinavian girls in tight shorts and orange backpacks trudging along the tree-shaded avenue. "Do you suppose those young ladies could use a ride?" he said half to himself. He leaned forward to tap the glass behind the driver's head but was stopped by his secretary's soft cough.

"Jamshid Ansari is a member of the Muslim Marxist Alliance, Your Excellency, and could be associated with the propaganda about the Twelfth Imam."

The minister subsided in his seat and stared quizzically at his secretary. "How do you know that?"

"To compile my report I wrote to some of your followers who I thought might know something. One reply I received was from a student who is both a believer in your philosophy and a member of the Muslim Marxist Alliance."

"Marx would spin in his grave if he could hear my ideas," said Hormozi with a smile. "I'm amazed that anyone could be so stupid as to believe in both of us. Go on, though; I'm listening."

"What he said in his letter was that members of the alliance have been given handbills to post on walls and in public buildings. He enclosed one of them. Essentially, it says that the end of time is near and that the Shah is the prophesied Beast who will be destroyed when the Hidden Imam returns."

"What a bunch of rot."

"He also said that the chairman of the alliance at his university is Jamshid Ansari."

"Ahhh, the connection. Do you think Mr. Ansari knows that one of his cell members is writing such letters? No, I suppose he doesn't. Perhaps Mr. Ansari has come to recruit my support, then. That could be very interesting."

The remainder of the distance to the ministry was covered in silence. Abbas Azad didn't wish to disturb the minister's thoughts, but he also didn't wish to appear idle. Accordingly, he fixed his eyes squarely on the road ahead and watched the traffic hurtle past.

While Hormozi rapidly glanced through his secretary's report and chuckled over the messianic handbill with its sketch of the Twelfth Imam and inflammatory slogans, Jamshid Ansari was allowed to wait an additional hour. It would serve to impress upon him the value of the minister's time. Finally he was permitted to enter and cross the vast expanse of creamy Kirman carpet to the single visitor's chair near Hormozi's chrome-and-rosewood desk.

"Is this room safe from eavesdropping?" Jamshid asked.

"Entirely," replied Hormozi.

"What I am going to tell you, Dr. Hormozi, I am going to tell you for one reason alone: you are the only man in Iran who is entirely at home both in the modern scientific world and in the world of Islamic thought. That is very important to young people like myself. We admire you and look to you for leadership as we face the quandaries and challenges brought by rapid economic development."

Hormozi lowered his head in a gesture that acknowledged the praise while simultaneously bidding the honeyed words to stop.

"You must not ask me how I know the things I am going to tell you. I will reveal nothing that will incriminate others." The minister's head lowered again. Jamshid had a feeling that his effort at sincerity was not having a very telling effect.

"Very good. Now, what is it you want to tell me?" Hormozi fixed his visitor with a dazzling smile.

Jamshid took a deep breath. "There is a plot being made to overthrow His Imperial Majesty." He exhaled fully. The minister waited for him to continue, the beaming smile gone. "I do not know when it is planned for the blow to strike, but it is being done in the name of the Twelfth Imam." Jamshid felt slightly uneasy. His revelations seemed to be producing little effect on the minister. "I also do not know the name of the person claiming to be the Twelfth Imam, if he truly exists at all; but I do know the identity of one of the conspirators. He is Ayatollah Pirzadeh, the rector of the Ja'fari Islamic Law College in Qom."

"Is that all?" asked the minister after a silence of several seconds.

"That is all I know," said his visitor. Jamshid decided that something had gone wrong. His eyes traced the intricacies of interlaced roses on the carpet while his mind raced. Denouncing Pirzadeh was a calculated risk, but it had seemed a safer course than waiting for the bloodthirsty mulla to decide that he was no longer useful. The coup might still go ahead without the Ayatollah; and, if not, there was always a next time.

Hormozi allowed Jamshid to stare at the floor for several minutes to let the psychological pressure build. He relished the situation. The naming of a person as prominent as Ayatollah Pirzadeh had truly shocked him, but he had successfully controlled his expression. Finally, he broke the silence with a harsh, booming voice.

"Do you take me for a fool, Jamshid Ansari? Do you think I do not know that you are a leader of the Muslim Marxist Alliance? Do you think that I am unaware of the plotting that you are doing? That *I* do not know of the treachery of Ayatollah Pirzadeh? There is nothing that happens in this country that His Imperial Majesty's government does not know. It is only His Imperial Majesty's benevolence that has permitted the freedom for these scurrilous plots to breed in." He could see that his bombastic attack was having its effect. The young Marxist was visibly trembling in his chair. "You must tell me fully of your part in this plot before I decide what action to take." Jamshid continued to stare at the carpet. "YOU MUST TELL ME NOW!" The shouted command straightened the accused in his chair.

"I will name no names," said Jamshid weakly.

Hormozi was suddenly sweetness again, but the iron behind the velvet voice could clearly be sensed. "Do not name names, then. Just tell me *your* part."

Unnerved by the unforeseen turn of events, Jamshid had difficulty looking the minister in the face. "My colleagues and I coordinate the actions of the groups on the left," he said at last in a voice scarcely above a whisper.

"What actions?"

"We carry out propaganda for the Twelfth Imam. We spread the message among the young people that the Twelfth Imam will destroy the Shah and bring progressive rule."

"What else?"

Jamshid didn't reply until the command was repeated in a sterner voice. "We are receiving materials from the Soviet Union. The arrangements were our responsibility."

"What materials?"

"Lightweight armor. It is something like fiberglass that comes in thick sheets."

"What's that for?" asked Hormozi with genuine curiosity.

"I don't know."

"Where is it to be delivered?"

"To Nishapur. It is needed for the appearance of the Twelfth Imam."

"In Nishapur? Why Nishapur? Is it to be at the tomb of Hossein Makfuf?"

"Yes, I think so."

"When?"

"During the Moharram ceremonies."

"Who is the Twelfth Imam?"

"I was telling the truth. I don't know. Ayatollah Pirzadeh told me that the Twelfth Imam entered Iran two months ago and is staying in Qom. That is all I know."

Hormozi suddenly found himself devoid of questions. His mind was jangling. More by instinct than by conscious decision he stifled an impulse to telephone Colonel Ziya. A sudden thought flashed through his head.

"Do you know Colonel Ziya?" he asked.

Jamshid looked utterly astonished. "That's the second time I've been asked that question. No, I don't know Colonel Ziya."

Hormozi's thoughts were were racing ahead. The vaguest glimmer of a stupendous idea was beginning to form. He drummed his fingers on the rosewood desk top. Then he returned his attention to Jamshid.

"Listen to me closely, Jamshid Ansari. You said you came to me because you thought I was the embodiment of a true Muslim in the modern world. I don't know whether you were being honest or not." He raised a finger to stifle any protestation. "In

83

any case, the fact that you decided to denounce Ayatollah Pirzadeh to me instead of to SAVAK indicates that you hoped to save your own skin. Pirzadeh is a threat to you, perhaps." Hormozi paused but got no response. "It doesn't matter. What matters is that you did come to me instead of going to SAVAK. That was wise. This is a religious affair, however dangerous it may be; and SAVAK does not understand religion. I do, however. And, because I do, I know that if we move too quickly to cut off the head of this threat, the body will grow a new and more dangerous head. Therefore, we must wait and find out more. You, Jamshid, shall find out more for me. In return, I shall delay telling SAVAK what you have told me."

Jamshid looked closely at the excited minister. Was it possible that he had been tricked into a confession? It made no difference; he had no choice. "I will do what you wish," he said firmly.

CHAPTER **12**

With the end of the Ramadan fast, work quickened in the ruins around the shrine of Hossein Makfuf. The medieval Nishapur that had been inhabited by over a hundred thousand people before succumbing to internecine conflict and invasion by Mongols had left several square miles of ruins. The succeeding centuries of summer winds and winter rains had combined to render individual structures totally amorphous. Undisturbed the site would have been no more than a barren expanse of softly rounded knolls and mounds. But the site had not been undisturbed. Material from the ruins was useful as fertilizer on the fields of the scattered peasant villages, and the digging for fertilizer had inevitably uncovered pottery and other buried objects that had been sold to antiquities dealers from Tehran who came through regularly to purchase the finds. This, in turn, had spawned a local treasure-hunting industry that had utilized traditional skills in well digging to mine the ruins. Several villages subsisted entirely on the proceeds of such nominally illegal digging. As a result, the ruins were a barren expanse of scarred and pockmarked terrain.

The work to turn the central part of the ruins into prayer grounds capable of accommodating tens of thousands of pilgrims would have gone quickly with bulldozers, but the only tools at hand were shovels, scoops, and heavy wooden sleds pulled by teams of oxen. Since it was the beginning of winter, ample peasant manpower was available for toiling in the crisp, cool air. The deep pits dug by treasure hunters were covered and partially filled, while the broader, shallower excavations from which fertilizer had been extracted were brought up to the level of the surrounding terrain by shoveling nearby hummocks of rubble into them.

Ben Groves checked the progress of the work almost daily and spoke frequently about the plans with his short custodian friend from the Hossein Makfuf shrine. The plans seemed incomplete and chaotic; but as weeks passed it became possible to discern the emergence of an enormous rectangle that was appreciably flatter and less encumbered with pits and clumps of ruins than what lay outside it. At the same time, the path from the Hossein Makfuf shrine, which was in the middle of the long east side of the rectangle, to the dirt road was widened and graded. Groves was told that before Moharram the dirt road itself would be graded and graveled. Another path was simultaneously being built from the middle of the long western side of the rectangle to the magnificent shrine of Mohammad Mahruq a kilometer away.

In a particularly visionary moment the diminutive shrine custodian took Groves to the middle of the developing rectangle and gestured sweepingly toward the center of the west side. There, he explained, was where the great platform would be erected from which the eloquent mullas would preach to the masses. On either side of the platform would be the long closed tents for the women, from which they could hear the words of the sermons but not interfere with the men's pious activities. Groves noted that it would be impossible for the women to see anything, but his guide had already passed on to contemplating the area in front of the platform. Groves was told that would be maintained as an open area where performers would enact the pathetic drama of the martyrdom of Hossein Makfuf. Groves made a mental note to ask questions later; no such drama existed; and if one was being written, it would be essential for him to procure the script. For the moment he tried to empathize with the custodian's vision of fifty thousand praying, weeping men standing in a packed mass in the narrow northern and southern ends of the rectangle and along the eastern side in front of the humble shrine of Hossein Makfuf. The number seemed impossibly large, but there was certainly room for many thousands of worshipers.

The shrine itself would, of course, be rebuilt on a magnificent scale from the donations of the pilgrims; and Groves could tell from the visionary description of the future edifice that his guide anticipated becoming its custodian as well. Until after Moharram, however, the shrine would remain as it was. There would only be built in front of it a temporary low platform, much lower than the one on the opposite side, which would be covered with awnings and furnished with chairs to accommodate government officials and distinguished visitors.

Groves was impressed, and not a little awestruck, that *his* discovery had set the giant enterprise in motion. Despite its present chaotic appearance, he was willing to believe that the site would be ready in time according to plan. Nor was it simply that he was carried away by the little mulla's rhapsodizing. His conversations with the Chief of Education and a number of other city officials had already revealed to him the depth of planning behind the great event, including a huge vacant area near the railroad station which had been marked up for future construction of a tent city, the tents to be provided by the Imperial Iranian Gendarmerie. Pipes would be laid to bring water to a dozen points in the tent city, and businessmen from the pilgrimage city of Mashhad, only two hours distant, had been called in to give advice on provisioning the expected throng with foodstuffs and other necessaries, advice drawn from years of catering to a comparable influx of worshipers to their own city.

At the end of his soliloquy on the great pilgrimage, the custodian was dry enough and exhilarated enough to invite Groves to come and take tea with him in the garden of the Mohammad Mahruq shrine. The honor was gratefully accepted, and as they walked the kilometer from the prayer grounds to the great domed shrine along the freshly leveled dirt path, the custodian described to him how in less than three months a procession of great religious and lay dignitaries would be making their way in a stately manner in the opposite direction to preside over the worshipful rites. Groves had heard several of the names before and let his companion know that he was impressed. Only one name really interested him, however.

He interrupted the recitation to inquire, "Why is Dr. Mohammad Hormozi going to attend?"

The mulla leaned his turbaned head back to look up at the American's face. "He's the Minister of Culture and Art. I mentioned that."

"Yes, I know that he's the Minister of Culture and Art. But he surely does not attend all religious gatherings in Moharram."

The custodian had stopped and taken his arm to help explain things to him. "This is not like other pilgrimages." His eyes began to get a visionary look again.

"No, of course not," said Groves hastily. "This is entirely different, the celebration of the miracle of the discovery of the tomb of Hossein Makfuf. But, as you know, the government has not officially confirmed the authenticity of the miracle."

The custodian sneered. "God does not need the government's approval." He was visibly restraining himself from saying more, and just as visibly his restraint gave way, and an enthusiastic tumble of words came out. "You must tell no one this. I am telling you only because you were the instrument of God's miracle in revealing the tomb."

"What are you telling me?"

"That the Minister of Culture and Art is coming in person to tell the pilgrims that the tomb is genuine and lead them in prayer. He will be with the mullas as well as with the government officials."

Groves looked surprised. His personal knowledge of Hormozi did not jibe with seeing him in an austere brown robe and white turban.

"This is a secret because if it was known why he was coming everyone would know the government's conclusion on the tombstone. He does not want anyone to know until he makes his speech."

"I shall tell no one," said Groves solemnly as they reached the gate to the shrine's garden.

The air out in the ruins had been crisp and cool, but the bright sun had kept them warm. Under the fruit trees in the shrine's garden they quickly realized that it was too chilly to sit outside. Groves's host excused himself and said he would return in two minutes. He returned and, with a conspiratorial smile, informed Groves that the room in the shrine where the mullas took their tea was unoccupied and that he would risk taking him there where a nice kerosene stove made sipping tea more comfortable.

With almost comical stealth the short mulla and the gangling professor made their way into the shrine by a side door and then down a hallway past a busy kitchen to a small room furnished with pads and cushions on the floor and decorated with fine examples of religious sayings done in a bold and masterful calligraphic hand. The custodian seemed scandalously amused that he had actually brought a Christian into a place reserved for mullas, but he drank his tea with unseemly rapidity nonetheless. Groves took a minute longer to avoid scorching his mouth and had time to look more closely at an item of furniture partly hidden behind the door. It was a portable short-wave radio of an unusually elaborate kind. It looked remarkably like the one that had been in the van of the fat American economist, Freddy Desuze, who had given him the ride to Nishapur. Groves was sure it was the same exact model. What odd coincidences one encounters in foreign travel, he thought.

When he arrived back in town Groves saw for the first time a handbill proclaiming the imminent return of the Twelfth Imam. At the top was a line drawing of the Twelfth Imam with a blank veil in place of a face in the time-honored tradition of Iranian religious art. The printing was quite professional in appearance. The slogans themselves were inflammatory and said more about the Shah than about the Imam. However, what struck Groves as the strangest element on close scrutiny was the faint imprint in the paper itself of what looked like the emblem of the ruling party of Iraq.

CHAPTER 13

For the first week following his interview with Jamshid Ansari, Mohammad Hormozi suffered from unceasing mental agitation. He ate and slept little and even found his mind wandering during the crucial moment of a tryst with Susan Bengston. The second week saw some tentative conclusions emerge from his fevered mental activity. The outline of a plan of action began to take shape, and Abbas Azad was sent on an urgent mission to the immigration authority. Then, when he received the secretary's report, Hormozi closeted himself for half a day in the theological library of the central Tehran mosque. At the end of the week he reached a decision and took the dangerous step of telephoning Colonel Rahmatollah Ziya at SAVAK headquarters. The colonel sounded positively grandfatherly and expressed what seemed like real delight at the minister's suggestion that they lunch together.

Hormozi was slightly ahead of the agreed appointment time at the Tehran Officers Club. To his surprise, the colonel was already waiting for him in the plushly appointed lobby. They immediately went upstairs to the dining room. After an appetizer of the finest-grade Caspian caviar, Hormozi elected to try the duck with peaches, the chef at the Officers Club being noted for his Parisian training. To his surprise, Colonel Ziya passed up the list of Iranian dishes and also ordered from the French side of the menu: *rognons de veau bordelaise.* Noting the look on the minister's face, Ziya said that he had once been a military attaché to the embassy in Paris.

There was no pretense to serious discussion until the cheese plate had been served, accompanied by *café filtre.* Hormozi had eaten in the Officers Club on two previous occasions and had found that admiring comments on what had grown to be one of the attractive privileges of being a member of the Iranian officer corps were well received. The white-haired colonel was suitably appreciative but took exception to his guest's mention that he had not known that SAVAK officers were members of the club. Without elaboration he remarked that his rank of colonel was a military one and that SAVAK officers were, indeed, ineligible for membership.

Seeing that his host was not inclined to press him about his reason for suggesting the lunch, Hormozi decided there was no advantage to be gained by just hinting at his business. So he broached the subject directly.

"Two and a half months ago, Colonel, you visited me with news of a plot against His Imperial Majesty and a request that the Ministry of Culture and Art find that the tombstone of Hossein Makfuf is genuine."

"I recall the visit vividly," said Ziya contentedly stroking his heavy white mustaches.

"As you can well imagine, I was alarmed by what you told me, alarmed at this threat to His Imperial Majesty by some sacrilegious impostor calling himself the Twelfth Imam, and concerned about how best to respond to your request regarding the tombstone."

The colonel produced two cigars from his uniform tunic. His guest refusing, he laid one of them on the tablecloth and ponderously set about with a pocket knife preparing the other for smoking. Hormozi was too experienced in the techniques of establishing dominance in a conversation to be impressed by the ritual demonstration of disinterest.

"With regard to my second concern, I wanted to inform you that I have made plans to announce my favorable decision regarding the tombstone's validity in person at the Moharram ceremonies being planned for Nishapur. I will speak in my religious capacity as well as my official one, of course." Hormozi detected a flicker of a pause in the slow ritual of lighting the cigar. "In addition, you may recall the theory of the American professor Benjamin Groves that the stone was recut after the destruction of the genuine stone in railway excavation. Nothing could be found at the Ministry of Railways that might prove or disprove the theory, but I have made provisions for appropriate records to be made and inserted in the archives confirming the theory. A decision not based upon documentary evidence might be challenged." He saw that, despite the colonel's pose of inattention, he was beginning to capture his interest.

"With regard to my alarm about the plot against His Imperial Majesty, I have become very attentive to any information that might help you in uncovering and destroying the conspiracy. Recently some thoughts have occurred to me that might be of assistance. First, the connection between the impostor calling himself the Twelfth Imam and the tomb of Hossein Makfuf is not an obvious one. I might suggest, however, that it is possible that the one claiming to be the Twelfth Imam intends to make himself known at the Moharram ceremonies in Nishapur. The conspirators could be planning to use the natural fervor of the ceremonies to their advantage. This would explain why they wish the stone to be found to be genuine. The opposite decision might cause the ceremonies to be canceled."

Hormozi deliberately stopped and took up the cigar lying on the tablecloth. Without haste he nipped off the tip with his teeth and patted his vest pockets for a match. Colonel Ziya was a trifle faster than a genuinely bored listener should have been in producing the gold lighter he had used on his own cigar.

"Now, it has also occurred to me, Colonel—for whatever my amateurish ideas may be worth—that the vile charlatan claiming to be the Twelfth Imam may actually claim to be or let himself be believed to be the reincarnation of Hossein Makfuf himself. I am sure you are aware that the popular cult that has arisen around the supposed tomb of Hossein Makfuf has claimed that the discovery of his tomb is a divine miracle. The conspirators might therefore plan to stage a second miracle to feed the credulity of the pious masses: a miraculous reappearance of the Twelfth Imam. Unfortunately," he eyed Ziya closely, "the consensus of centuries of scholarship by various sects on the question of the Hidden Imam is that he must be perfect in mind and body, besides being a direct descendant of the Imam Ali, may God be pleased with him. In other words, if a blind man posing as Hossein Makfuf should claim to be the Twelfth Imam, no mulla in Iran could believe the claim." The colonel's complete lack of reaction was a reaction in itself. "Hence, this second idea is probably incorrect," concluded Hormozi lightly as if he had finally succeeded in thinking through a complex problem.

Colonel Ziya inclined his heavy head in a respectful manner. "These are very serious ideas you have come upon, Dr. Hormozi. I must give them great thought. You have proven that I was correct when I called you one of our most profound Muslim thinkers when I visited you previously. My deepest thanks."

"One more small point, Colonel." The minister pulled a folded piece of paper from his inside coat pocket. "You surely have seen these handbills," he said as he unfolded the paper. The colonel nodded without looking. "I was sure it didn't escape your attention. I simply wanted to point out that the paper it's printed on appears to be from Iraq." With the long, filed nail of his little finger he indicated the faint outlines of a watermark. "Given our history of bad relations with our neighbor to the west, that could be an indicator of subversive activity."

"We are already looking into the matter," responded Ziya

with an air of finality. With that he slowly rose from his chair and guided the minister before him out of the large dining room, all the while repeating his thanks for the minister's aid and bidding him to report any additional ideas that might come to him.

As they went down the broad red-carpeted steps to the lobby, Hormozi was prompted by his previous train of conversation to ask his host what kind of miracle he thought might be staged to convince the pious of the Twelfth Imam's return. The question died in his mouth, however, as his gaze lit upon a glass case that was prominently situated in the lobby below.

Enshrined in the case was an elaborate dress uniform of an old design with heavy epaulettes and what appeared to be sticks passing through it. On a previous visit to the club the uniform had been reverently pointed out to him by a younger officer he had once gone to school with. It was the uniform that the Shah had been wearing when he had been shot at five times by a would-be assassin in 1949. The uniform was mounted as if a body were inside it, and the sticks passed through the entrance holes made by the bullets and out the exit holes. The impact of the display on anyone who saw it was always the same: the Shah's escape with only minor wounds had been truly miraculous. Judging from the uniform, the bullets must have passed through vital parts of his body without harming him. It could only be explained by a miracle.

Hormozi was so absorbed in the ideas stimulated by the sight of the Shah's uniform that he was almost inattentive to the colonel's leavetaking at the entrance to the club; but he pulled himself together enough to promise to keep SAVAK informed of any fresh thoughts he might have. Then his own pearl-gray-and-black Mercedes stopped before him and he slid with relief into the plush cocoon of the back seat.

Pushing the button that sealed him off from the driver, he resumed the thoughts that the final formalities with the colonel had interrupted. While he thought, he again extracted the folded handbill from his coat pocket. He stared vacantly at the line drawing of the veiled Imam. As the car neared the ministry, his vacant look of total concentration gave way to a broad smile. He extracted a silver felt-tipped pen from the opposite side of his coat and smoothed the handbill across his thigh. Quickly he drew a caricature of a face on top of the veil that concealed the holy visage of the Twelfth Imam. He made the eyes dark and penetrating, the nose straight and thin, the mustache dense but neatly trimmed, and the mouth set in a toothy smile. It was a caricature he had drawn many times before in a combination of self-mockery and self-admiration. He pressed the button to lower the window on the back of the front seat.

"I've changed my mind," he said to the driver. "Take me to the Iran-America Society." And, after Miss Bengston, Mr. Ansari, he added to himself.

At the next intersection the driver skillfully negotiated a U-turn in heavy traffic and redirected the car on a familiar route.

Despite being endowed with the wavy black hair, chiseled features, and clean profile of a romantic lead, Frank Quintana had always been perfectly content in supporting roles. Not only was his own career a model of propriety and reliability within a large bureaucracy, but he was not inclined to envy or admire unduly those who were spectacularly successful, like Bill Keller, or great in reputation, like Emmanuel Holachek. Nevertheless, a two-week crash course in the art and science of spying in the late twentieth century could not help but stir his imagination and stimulate fantasies of adventure and intrigue.

His instructors never ceased to stress that the quiet and methodical accumulation of publicly available or carefully decrypted information provided the most reliable intelligence. The image they projected of a successful spy was approximately that of an unostentatious certified public accountant. At the same time they were filling his head with exotic ways of sending and receiving messages in cipher, tricks of recording and storing information to minimize the possibility of detection, and instructions in the use of specialized communications equipment. At Ambassador Dermott's insistence the Department of State had vetoed special instruction in armed or unarmed combat, since formally Quintana would be on a normal assignment as an assistant vice-consul in Tehran, and this legal status would have to be fully substantiable if something should go sufficiently wrong to provoke a Congressional inquiry. The training he received, therefore, was not to be fundamentally different from the training a State Department foreign service officer could be legitimately, under some imaginable circumstances, expected to receive. The spirit of this ruling was violated only to the extent of instructing Quintana in surveillance and eavesdropping techniques that even the nosiest ambassador could not legitimately be expected to make use of.

By the time the fledgling spy landed at Mehrabad Airport and passed through customs into the great dismal barn that had been serving for years as a temporary waiting room, he was so filled with a hyper-awareness of his surroundings and the potential he suddenly felt they held for unrest and violence that he failed to notice the driver the embassy had sent to meet him until the man spoke to him. Frank gave a start but quickly satisfied himself that the driver was the genuine article and not someone sent to abduct him.

On the drive to the embassy Frank took note of the vast new construction projects that had sprung up around the Shahyad monument since his last tour three years previously. Just for practice, he also used a tiny pencil stub to jot down on a scrap of paper a few words describing his driver and the automobile without removing his hand from his coat pocket. When he pulled the paper out, he observed that he would have to work to perfect his alignment of words. The car was described as being black and bald, and the driver came out having a blue suit and four doors. He emitted a rueful sigh and hoped that his mission would not require him to use too many of his newly acquired skills.

When they arrived at the embassy, he was immediately

guided to the office of Ambassador Dermott. He knew that the ambassador had not approved of his assignment and that as a foreign-service officer he was still formally subject to embassy authority. Yet he also knew that Emmanuel Holachek had prevailed upon the Secretary of State to instruct the ambassador to cooperate. Little knowing what kind of reception he was about to receive, the good bureaucrat involuntarily gritted his teeth when the ambassador's secretary told him he could go in.

Frank's last previous visit to the magnificent office had been to receive a politely tepid bon voyage and thank you for services rendered from a stiff and colorless ambassador with a Yankee accent. The reception he got this time from a thick, florid diplomat with steely gray hair was neither stiff nor colorless. It was closer, in fact, to a Marine drill sergeant's reception of a new recruit.

"Young man," said the ambassador in a threatening voice after shaking his hand and pushing him into a chair in one continuous motion, "I utterly and completely disapprove of what you have been sent here to do." Frank had to swivel his head to follow the diplomat's pacing. "I realize that you have been sent here under orders; I have my orders, as well. Nevertheless, you certainly would not have been sent if you had not consented to—I might even say asked for—the assignment. I do not by any means consider you an innocent in this affair. If anything happens to cast the slightest cloud over our relations with Iran, or the slightest disgrace on this embassy, I shall not hesitate one second in naming you in my report. You cannot hide behind the skirts of the National Security Advisor and that boy wonder of his." His contempt for Emmanuel Holachek and Bill Keller was obvious. "You are as responsible as they are for whatever might happen. Is that clear?"

"Yes, Sir."

"Don't interrupt me. Within the limits of my instructions from the secretary I have devised certain rules that you are to live by while you are here in Iran. First, you will involve no one else from this embassy in any act that is inappropriate for a foreign service officer. I assume you still recollect what sorts of things I am referring to. Second, you will keep the embassy fully informed about your whereabouts at all times. What you do is outside my jurisdiction, but I don't have to tolerate your running off without telling anyone the way Desuze used to do. And third, *all*—I repeat, *all*—communications to any department or agency in Washington must be simultaneously communicated to me personally or to anyone I designate. You are a foreign service officer, and I am your superior. I hope you will keep that well in mind."

"I will, Sir."

"Good. Welcome to Tehran. Now get the hell out of my office."

"As bad as that," said Susan Bengston matter of factly to Frank as they sat over coffee. "I've heard of him getting pretty hot, but I've never heard of him kicking anyone out of his office."

"Was he this way with Freddy Desuze?"

"With Freddy? I don't think so. Everybody got along just fine with Freddy. He was known as the Fat Spook." Susan had been informed by cable from the CIA that Frank Quintana would be continuing Freddy Desuze's investigation and that she should give him the same sort of assistance she had given his predecessor.

"Well, he really has it in for me. I haven't been talked to that way since I was cut from the football team in high school."

Susan Bengston was rather taken with the cautious bureaucratic mentality hiding behind Frank's romantic exterior. "Perhaps he's simply upset about Freddy's death and worried about the same thing happening to you." The sickish look on Frank's face told her she had brought up an unfortunate subject. "Well, perhaps you should tell me what I can do to help you," she said quickly.

"Oh, yes." Frank returned from a bad daydream. "I read in

100

the report on Freddy's death that you had spoken to him about Dr. Hormozi and the Hossein Makfuf cult. You don't have to tell me what it's all about; I'm only too familiar with it. But is there anything else you can remember mentioning to him that might be important?"

There was no hesitation before answering. "I've thought about that again and again. He wanted to know whether Mohammad—that's Dr. Hormozi—was preoccupied with any special business. I mentioned that he sometimes gets tense about his radio sermons, and Freddy said that wasn't important. Then I remembered about the tomb business. I said there was a cult based on something Professor Groves had discovered in Nishapur. He said he remembered Groves because he had driven him to Nishapur."

"Desuze drove Ben Groves to Nishapur? And Groves is in Iran now?"

"Yes, of course. He's here on an NEH grant to study the Hossein Makfuf cult. He and Freddy met at a reception at the Iran-America Society just a day or so before Freddy was scheduled to drive to Mashhad. He offered Groves a ride, and off they went."

"Just the two of them all the way to Nishapur?"

"I suppose just the two of them. I never asked."

"None of this was mentioned in the report."

"That's because it wasn't really what Freddy and I were talking about that night. I used Groves's name to describe this cult; Freddy was just picking up on it because it was the name of someone he had met. What interested Freddy was Dr. Hormozi's involvement and the possibility that SAVAK and the palace disagreed over the issue of the tomb's genuineness."

"But Groves was talked about. You're sure of that."

"Of course I'm sure," said Susan testily. "If you're thinking he went to see Professor Groves after talking to me, however, you might consider that it's over a two-day drive from Nishapur to where his car was found in that canyon on the Ab-i Ali road."

"He still might have learned something important from

Groves on their earlier trip that would provide a clue to what he did after he left you."

Susan eyed him skeptically. "I can see you don't really know Professor Benjamin Groves. He's not the sort of man you learn something important from. I don't think he knows Iran has political problems, or even that there are people who dislike the Shah's government."

"But I do know Professor Groves," replied Frank with a smile. "I took a course from him in graduate school." He paused for effect. "And your analysis of him is absolutely correct."

Susan smiled graciously at what was clearly intended as a subtle compliment.

"One final thing," Frank continued. "Has anything come up since Freddy's death that might tie in with Hormozi or Groves or Hossein Makfuf?"

"Just one thing that I came across two days ago. You probably know that propaganda about the Twelfth Imam returning to overthrow the Shah had begun to appear in various cities. Well, I found this handbill on the floor of my office after a visit from Mohammad. It must have slipped out of his coat pocket." She looked Frank in the eye. "We're lovers, as I'm sure you are aware." Frank blushed. "It's one of the ordinary handbills, but look at what he's drawn on the veil."

Frank peered at the creased piece of paper. "It's a face."

"Not just a face; it's Mohammad's face. It's his standard caricature of himself. I've seen it dozens of times. He sometimes uses it in place of a signature to sign notes."

"And here it is on the veil of the Twelfth Imam," murmured Frank quizzically. He looked up. "You don't think he's the one calling himself the Twelfth Imam, do you? Minister of Culture and Art isn't much of a power base to stage a coup from."

"I don't know what to think," said Susan. "It's not a doodle, though. He only draws this when he's thinking of himself. Still, I can't see Mohammad as a revolutionary. I'm sure he'd like to run the country, but he wouldn't want to risk getting his shoes dirty."

"Sounds like a splendid man."

"He has his good points."

Frank looked up again from studying the cartoon. Susan's face had a defiant quality about it. Very fair blondes had seldom appealed to him because they seemed to have so little character, but he sensed that under the right conditions he could grow to like Susan Bengston very much. The conditions he had in mind, however, did not include a dashing Iranian cabinet minister who made office visits that involved laying his coat on the floor.

"I think I should go out to Nishapur and talk to Professor Groves."

"Don't forget to tell Ambassador Dermott. I expect he'll be happy to have you safely out of Tehran."

"You think it's a waste of time, don't you."

"Of course. But what do I know? I'm not the highly trained secret agent you are."

Dhu al-Qa' da: The Fourth Month

CHAPTER 15

A flatbed trailer truck was an unusual sight on Nishapur's main street. The railroad had been built to follow the traditional caravan route linking the string of cities east of Tehran that were situated just south of the long eastward arc of the Elburz Mountains and just north of the great desert that occupied most of central Iran. It had superseded the caravan route as their primary means of communication and access to markets.

Since the railroad could be competitively undermined by a good modern highway following the same route, however, most of the old road had been left unpaved while a first-class asphalt highway was carved out of the rugged terrain on the northern side of the mountains. All that was left on the road south of the mountains was short-distance interurban traffic and long-distance passenger buses.

However, even the rarity of a flatbed trailer truck did not make it an object of interest to Nishapur's inhabitants. Few heads lifted to observe its passage, and few eyes followed its course through town and out the eastern side in the direction of Mashhad. Two exceptions to this general indifference were Professor Benjamin Groves, standing in front of the cream-colored Ministry of Culture and Art building, and Zhaleh Hekmat, waiting impatiently at the Omar Khayyam traffic circle. Ben Groves noticed the truck and wondered idly where it was taking the thick sheets of construction materials with which it was loaded. He also noted that the design of the truck was not a familiar one and wondered where it was coming from.

Zhaleh Hekmat was waiting to flash a signal to the driver whether to turn off on the road to the Mohammad Mahruq shrine or continue innocently on to Mashhad. Since nothing had happened during her two crushingly tedious months in the provincial city to make her suspect that the conspiracy had been detected, she produced the agreed-upon red cloth from beneath her chadur and shook it as the truck drove by. Two kilometers further on, the view from town was obstructed by the trees planted along the sides of the road, and the big dusty truck geared down to make an abrupt right-hand turn. It turned again onto a newly graded and graveled road that departed from the left side of the paved road just before it rose to cross the railroad tracks. After that it was lost in a cloud of dust, but only one destination was possible: the broad, flat rectangular prayer grounds that had been laboriously constructed next to the tiny white shrine of Hossein Makfuf.

Having performed her first duty, Zhaleh walked excitedly to the city's central intersection and turned left. The Post, Telephone, and Telegraph building was a short way down the street, half the distance to the railroad station. She went up the steps and entered beneath the red PTT sign in Persian and Latin characters. Only a few steps ahead of her was Ben Groves, who had been strolling slowly in the same direction from his much nearer starting point near the central intersection. The urgency of Zhaleh's steps was explained by the message contained in the code words she planned to transmit by telegram to an address in Tehran: CARGO ARRIVED SAFELY. Groves's lassitude, on the other hand, was simply the product of his meager expectation of there being anything in his box worth looking at. With no close family and few friends who qualified as more than mediocre correspondents, Groves's sparse mail usually consisted of departmental business from his home university.

Glancing through the three envelopes his visit had yielded and noticing that one bore the return address of the U.S. embassy in Tehran, Groves was about to leave when he noticed Zhaleh filling out a form at the telegraph window. He sidled a few steps closer to get a good look at her face within the oval frame of her chadur. There could be no question that it was the same woman he had seen get off the bus two months before. Although he had caught sight of her from a distance in the bazaar a few times since then, this was the first time he had been able to observe her closely. He was immediately struck by the fact that she was unusually pretty. The dark eyes, heavy eyebrows, and full mouth that were typical of so many Iranian women were uncommonly, almost classically, harmonious; and the angular set of her cheek and jaw contrasted strikingly with the more customary Iranian ideal of the moon-faced maiden.

Groves felt his dormant curiosity in the woman reviving. When he had first taken an interest in her in the chelo kebab restaurant near the bus stop, he had assumed that the ensuing weeks would afford the opportunity to find out who she was, but his assumption had proved wrong. Discreet inquiries of his friend, the custodian of the Hossein Makfuf shrine, had elicited the information that she was a servant at the Mohammad Mahruq shrine, where she also lived. This reduced enormously the chances of his getting to talk to her, and the chances fell to zero when the little mulla further informed him that someone had reported their taking tea together inside the shrine. As a consequence of this breach of etiquette, Groves would no longer be welcome within or on the grounds of the Mohammad Mahruq shrine. Since that time, the brief glimpses he had had of the young woman in the bazaar had been insufficient to maintain his interest.

He had never been convinced that she was only a servant, but there was nothing he could do about it. Now, in the post office, his curiosity was renewed both by her beauty, which lacked the fleshy sturdiness of the usual local servants from peasant villages, and by the fact that she had been filling out a telegram form. Groves knew that exceptionally few servants could be counted as literate. He feverishly tried to think of a ploy to open a conversation with the young woman and even followed her out of the post office in hopes that a good idea would come to mind. Nothing came. Reluctantly, he slacked his pace and watched her disappear from sight down the crowded sidewalk.

Filled with regret at his failure to exploit a promising opportunity, Groves retraced his steps past the post office and up the secondary wall-flanked street that ran beside it. Nothing distinguished the wall around Mr. Kamel's courtyard from any other save the tiny official blue plaque that displayed its street number. Mr. Kamel himself unbolted the gate in answer to Groves's push on the buzzer.

"Oh, Professor Groves, a message for you a few minutes ago arrived."

"What kind of message?" said Groves as he stooped through the low gateway and descended the two steps to the brick-paved courtyard.

"It was from the office of the Chief of Education. It said that you are not permitted to go to Hossein Makfuf shrine some more."

Groves stopped in his tracks on the path toward the house. "Not permitted? Why not?"

"I do not know, Professor Groves," said Mr. Kamel obsequiously.

Groves glared at the slightly cowering schoolteacher and turned on his heel. There was only one place to go to resolve this type of difficulty.

Realizing the necessity for taking a forceful stance, Groves strode into the Ministry of Culture and Art building and up the stairs to the chief's office without going through any of the minor functionaries he would normally have spoken to. As usual, the chief's office was full of petitioners and flunkies. Groves ignored them and went directly to the chief's desk, where he towered over the dark little man.

"Why am I not permitted to go to Hossein Makfuf, Mr. Borumand?" His tone was stern but not belligerent. The belligerence could come later.

"I am sorry, Professor Groves," replied the chief, his eyes full of sympathy. "It is out of my hands. I pleaded for you to be allowed to continue, but I could do nothing."

"Pleaded with whom? Who is responsible?"

"It is a religious matter. The mullas at the shrine of Mohammad Mahruq have complained that you are trespassing on land that is a religious endowment. There is nothing I can do."

"Now listen to me, Mr. Borumand," said Groves belligerently. "I have traveled eight thousand miles to carry out this study, and I have obtained all necessary permission from the government. What is more, if it weren't for my discovery, the shrine of Hossein Makfuf would not even exist. I have no intention of stopping my visits to the shrine. Do you understand? All questions of religious endowments are in the hands of the Religious Endowments Authority in Tehran, as you well know." He was punctuating his remarks with a fist on the chief's desk. "Unless you produce an order from the Endowments Authority, I shall not stop my work. And, if you do produce such an order, I shall request my good and dear friend Dr. Hormozi, the Minister of Culture and Art, to dismiss you from your post." A final louder thump terminated the speech. The office was silent as the assorted flunkies and petitioners engaged their eyes elsewhere while keeping close track with their ears of what was being said.

Groves could see that his final threat had badly disconcerted the Chief. "Perhaps I could talk to the mullas once again, Professor Groves. Occasional visits might be specially arranged."

"No," shouted Groves. "My permission comes from the government, not from the mullas at Mohammad Mahruq. I shall continue to go wherever I need to go to do my work; and if you have me arrested, you will find out very quickly what kind of influence I have in Tehran."

The chief was thoroughly cowed. "It is out of my hands," he replied in a small voice.

Groves gave the ill-shaven little man a final glare and stalked out of the room. Not until he was in the street on his way back to Mr. Kamel's house did he permit a smile to crease his craggy countenance. He had enjoyed himself thoroughly. His only regret was that he would not be present to hear Mr. Borumand making up excuses for the mullas.

CHAPTER **16**

After leaving the post office, Zhaleh Hekmat had headed directly back toward the Omar Khayyam traffic circle. The sidewalk was crowded since recently installed railings prevented pedestrians from spreading out into the street as was their custom. Without warning an unseen man suddenly poked her from behind and spoke in a whisper next to her right ear.

"Zhaleh, it's Jamshid. Turn into the bazaar."

In an instant the man had pushed on past and moved off down the sidewalk, turning right into the covered bazaar. From behind she couldn't recognize him. Neither the slouching gait nor the cheap, workman's clothing fit her image of the sophisticated chief of the Muslim Marxist Alliance. The build and apparent age were right, however, and she followed him into the bazaar without hesitation.

Not knowing what was expected of her, Zhaleh kept her distance from the man ahead, stopping to look at the goods displayed in the open stalls whenever he did. Gradually, they worked their way through the crowded covered part of the bazaar and out on the south side, where a few humbler shops sold second-hand goods and junk. The man in the workman's clothing took a turn to the left down a narrow alleyway; Zhaleh turned after him and saw him dawdle at a courtyard door before ducking inside. She approached the doorway with a rising feeling of apprehension, but when she peered inside, the face looking back at her was unquestionably Jamshid's, albeit partially disguised by a few days' growth of beard and a pair of gold-rimmed glasses. He beckoned her inside and closed the door behind her.

"What . . ."

He put a finger on her lips. "Not here. Let's go inside." They crossed the small courtyard with its minute garden and solitary, bare fruit tree and entered the ramshackle house. Cushions, mats, and a low table made up the only furnishings in the simple main room.

"Whose house is this? What are you doing here? You're supposed to stay away from Nishapur. Has something gone wrong?"

Jamshid sank down on two cushions and removed the glasses. "We can't stay long. I don't want you to be missed at the shrine. But there has been a change in plans. You had to be consulted. There was no other way but to come here."

Zhaleh sat down on the opposite side of the room and eyed him warily. "What kind of change of plans?" she asked coldly.

Jamshid sighed. Zhaleh had never been an easy person to deal with. "We have been exchanging information with Dr. Hormozi."

"That jackass? Why would we do such a thing? How did he find out about us?"

"He's not a jackass. Many of our members respect his religious views. You know that as well as I do."

"Many of our members couldn't tell Mohammad from Marx if they were standing in front of them. And you know *that* perfectly well, Jamshid."

"Look, we don't have time to argue. The fact of the matter is that we are now working with Hormozi."

"What about Ayatollah Pirzadeh?"

"Pirzadeh was planning to betray us." He could see the news hit her face like a slap. "Hormozi figured it all out."

"I don't believe it."

"I know you don't. But just let me explain. Pirzadeh and the other mullas are working with a SAVAK colonel named Rahmatollah Ziya, who's apparently a very religious old man who came up under the Shah's father. Their plan is to stage the return of the Twelfth Imam and then use their religious authority to discredit the movement and help quell the revolt. We and the entire left are to be sacrificed and made the scapegoats. That's why Pirzadeh ordered us to get that truckload of armor material sent from the Soviet Union. SAVAK will have a record of that shipment all the way from the border to Nishapur. That's also why the propaganda we've been helping them hand out is printed on Iraqi paper. They want the whole thing to look like a Communist plot. As soon as they blow the whistle, we and everyone else on the left get arrested; but Pirzadeh and the mullas get credit from the Shah for saving the throne. At the same time they demonstrate to him how dangerous a religious revolt can be. This leaves the implied threat that, if he doesn't take their advice and show more respect for religion from now on, they might support a revolt the next time just as they did in 1906."

Zhaleh started to respond, stopped, and then started again. "This sounds like just a theory, Jamshid. Where's the proof? Why couldn't Pirzadeh be telling us the truth? You told us at the meeting of the Central Committee when we agreed to cooperate with him that you thought he genuinely hated the Shah."

"And I still believe he does. But, if a real religious revolution failed, it could be the end of everything for the mullas. To have a fake revolution and get the credit for stopping it is almost a sure thing, particularly when you have the cooperation of one of the SAVAK big shots to keep things from going wrong."

"Still, Jamshid, there's the matter of *proof.* Hormozi is such a fake he may have just made all this up."

"Well, he didn't make up Colonel Ziya. Even the CIA knows he's involved."

"How do you know that?"

"I'll tell you some other time," said Jamshid hastily. "The real proof is that Hormozi figured out who Pirzadeh's Twelfth Imam is going to be." He paused to let the words sink in. "It's a blind mulla named Hossein Sadr. Hormozi was trying to find out what the connection was between the Hossein Makfuf cult and the Twelfth Imam, and on a hunch he got a list from the immigration authority of all blind men named Hossein who crossed the border into Iran during the month of Sha'ban. There were fifteen names on the list, and one of them was a mulla named Hossein Sadr from Sanandaj who crossed over from Iraq at Khorramshahr. Hormozi telephoned the Chief of Education in Sanandaj to find out if he knew Hossein Sadr. The chief told him that he was a kind of crazy mystic who had gotten it into his head after the tombstone was discovered that he was the reincarnation of Hossein Makfuf. He's blind just as Hossein Makfuf was, you see. Hossein Sadr left Sanandaj over a year ago to go to Iraq and visit the shrines at Najaf and Kerbela. Hormozi's theory is that the entire plot was dreamed up by the mullas in Kerbela after meeting this man. Hormozi thinks they've convinced him that he really is the Twelfth Imam."

"That still doesn't prove Pirzadeh was lying to us, though. This crazy mulla could just be a figurehead who will be gotten rid of after the coup." Zhaleh's voice was calmly rational.

"True, and that might be the case—except for one thing: the Twelfth Imam has to be perfect in mind and body. A blind man *can't* be the Twelfth Imam. Hormozi thinks the mullas in Kerbela have convinced Hossein Sadr that when God reveals him to be the Twelfth Imam at the Moharram ceremonies his sight will be miraculously restored. But actually, as soon as he reveals

116

himself, every mulla in the country will denounce him because he's blind. The people follow the mullas; the revolt fails; and we are made the scapegoats." He could see his words taking effect on Zhaleh. "How is that for proof?"

"I don't know. I just don't know," she said. "It all sounds possible, but I can't believe that Ayatollah Pirzadeh would betray us. He's known as a man of honor. I thought he was convinced that Marxism and Islam could work together."

"Hormozi also discovered through the gendarmerie that, after Hossein Sadr returned to Iran, he walked all the way to Qom and then stayed there for a couple of months at the Ja'fari Law College. Rector: Ayatollah Pirzadeh." There was a long silence.

"What can we do?" said Zhaleh despairingly. "We are already completely incriminated."

"There is one chance, Zhaleh, and it is a good one as long as we have the will to make it work. Dr. Hormozi must become the Twelfth Imam."

"Hormozi! But that's impossible," she replied incredulously.

"It may be, but it's the only way. Hormozi feels that there is only one miracle that would convince the pilgrims at the Moharram ceremonies that Hossein Sadr is the Twelfth Imam. He must survive an assassination attempt without being harmed."

"Like the Shah . . ." she trailed off.

"Exactly. And not just the Shah either. Back in the fifties the Turkish Prime Minister Menderes survived a plane crash, and millions of Turks regarded it as a sign that he was chosen by God to be Prime Minister."

"So you think an assassination is going to be staged in order to create a miracle, is *that* it? And that's what the armor is for?"

"Precisely. Here in Nishapur during the Moharram ceremonies. Our hope is that if we know exactly what is planned and what the timing is it might be possible to substitute Dr. Hormozi for Hossein Sadr."

"You mean kidnap the blind man?"

"Or kill him."

"But wouldn't the mullas denounce Hormozi the same way they're planning to denounce Hossein Sadr?"

"No. That's why the plan might work. Hormozi is fully qualified to be the Twelfth Imam."

"Except for being a jackass."

"He's a sayyid descended directly from Ali; he's an established religious leader; and he's sound of mind and body. If the substitution can be made and he survives a staged assassination, the pilgrims will believe he is the Twelfth Imam, and the mullas won't have any basis for denying it. They'll have to go along."

"But this is ridiculous, Jamshid! How can a substitution be arranged? That blind man will surely be guarded, and we don't even know what the plans are."

"Think of the alternative, Zhaleh," said Jamshid. "If this doesn't work, we're dead, and our movement is dead. If it does, we have a stronger hold on the Twelfth Imam than we ever would have had by Pirzadeh's plan."

"I can't believe Hormozi has the spine to take such a risk himself. His ambition must be incredible."

"His risk isn't so great as it seems. Ours is. Up until the last minute Hormozi can pull out, and nothing will be left to incriminate him except our testimony; and that's not likely to count for much. He will be coming to the ceremonies anyway to announce the government's decision that the tombstone is genuine. It's up to us to find out how to make the substitution and convince him to go through with it. It's our only chance."

A light dawned in Zhaleh's face. "And that is to be my job? To find out what is planned? I can't do it, Jamshid. The mullas at the shrine hate me. They won't speak to me. I don't even have freedom to move around without saying where I'm going. It's been hell being here for two months."

"You must find a way, Zhaleh. You're the only one who can do it. I don't dare come here myself. I'm hardly an expert at disguises. The Central Committee is counting on you."

"The Central Committee?"

"Yes. I have informed them of everything, and they have voted unanimously to support Dr. Hormozi." He paused and then continued. "They've also voted to do something else, but we must have your cooperation on it, as well."

"What is it?" queried Zhaleh cautiously.

"Dr. Hormozi wants us to assassinate the Shah." For a long time Zhaleh did not respond; then she shook her head. "I know Pirzadeh reasoned that the revolution would lose the support of the people if the Shah were killed, but Dr. Hormozi says that's all part of Pirzadeh's plot to betray us. He said he would only cooperate if the Shah were killed, and he asked me whether we could do it. I told him I would have to consult the committee. I'm here to ask you, Zhaleh, whether you will agree." He looked steadily into her large dark eyes. "You know what I'm talking about, Zhaleh."

She nodded. "David."

"Will you contact him? We are all dead if you refuse, Zhaleh."

"You said you would never ask me to do this, Jamshid." Her voice was near breaking.

"I never thought I would have to. But now I must. Will you send him a telegram?"

At long length the girl nodded.

"Good. Tell David how to contact me. I must return to Tehran immediately and make the arrangements with Hormozi. I've already been here for three days waiting to get a chance to talk to you. I hope I can get back to Tehran without Pirzadeh's men recognizing me. It would raise suspicions. I'll leave first. Can you make up a story to explain why you were away from the shrine so long?"

"Yes," said Zhaleh blankly, her mind far away.

Jamshid was standing by the poorly fitted door. "By the way, you asked whose house this is. I flew to Mashhad and took a taxi from there, but before I left, I asked around the bazaar until I found someone who had come in from Ni-

119

shapur. This is his house. I rented it for three months for more money than he could make in a year." The girl did not appear to be listening. "I only mention it in case we ever need a safe place to meet again." She did not reply. "I'm sorry, Zhaleh. I'm truly sorry." He disappeared through the doorway.

CHAPTER 17

Frank Quintana had driven to Nishapur. As Susan Bengston had predicted, the ambassador had been happy to get him out of Tehran and had found a suitably durable vehicle for his use without undue delay. Still, the trip had been a time-consuming one. The distance was long, and the constant vibration of the washboard gravel surface had caused an electrical malfunction in the car that had eaten up a full day in Damghan as he waited for repairs to be completed. Nevertheless, Frank was not sorry he had chosen the slow means of transportation. If he had flown to Mashhad instead, he could have gotten to Nishapur much more quickly, but he would have been immobilized there if the need arose for further travel. Few vehicles were available for hire in provincial Iranian towns. In addition, Frank liked the desert landscape he had driven through, with the dry gravelly plain spreading endlessly away to the south and the low, multicolored mountains rising to the north.

Having checked into Nishapur's only decent hotel, a small, newly built concrete structure with fifteen rooms and a still rather pathetic garden, he had gone to speak to the Chief of Education. The little man seemed unhappy at the mention of Professor Groves's name, but he had told Quintana how to find the house of Mahmud Kamel, where Groves was staying.

Someone, whom Quintana judged to be a maid, refused to open the courtyard door when he rang, but in answer to his questions shouted through the thick wooden barrier she informed him that the American would be back at dinnertime. This left some three hours to kill, and one of them was more than sufficient to tour central Nishapur and confirm an initial observation that it contained nothing of interest. Even its bazaar was lacking in any sort of specialty that could not be found in any other provincial bazaar.

A second hour was spent driving out to the Omar Khayyam monument and the shrine of Mohammad Mahruq. The garden of the latter was closed to non-Muslims, but a fence instead of a wall separated the shrine garden from the one around the Omar Khayyam monument, so an excellent view of the beautiful seventeenth-century tiled dome and entrance archway was still available. By comparison, the monument to Nishapur's famous poet was not terribly impressive, even though its subtle parabolic curves and tile mosaic of lines of poetry were much more interesting to look at than the usual run of twentieth-century Iranian artwork. Moreover, the garden was uncommonly attractive, even at the dead time of year, with large trees and banks of dormant flowerbeds. The modern, well-built motel-like structure across the road from the garden puzzled Quintana, but a gardener informed him that it was the official guesthouse of the Shah. He also pointed out two large square areas of cement marked with yellow circles behind the guesthouse: helicopter landing pads.

Pondering what to do to occupy the third hour, Frank considered driving through the ruins of the medieval city which could be seen spreading out to the east of the Omar Khayyam monument. The helpful gardener told him where to find the road that led in that direction, but when Quintana arrived at the

122

turnoff onto the newly graveled side road; he found that a chain had been strung across it. Left with no other choice, he drove on back into the city and idled away the remainder of the time reading an Agatha Christie mystery in his hotel room. Exactly three hours after his first visit, Frank showed up again at the Kamel house.

"Your letter telling me you were coming beat you here by three days," said Ben Groves when they had shut themselves into Mr. Kamel's seldom-used reception room. Fifteen or more straight chairs lined the walls of the chilly, barren room, making it impossible to make oneself comfortable; but it was the one room in the house that gave assurance of privacy.

"I hope my coming isn't inconvenient. I don't know whether you recall me from your class or not. It must have been close to fifteen years ago."

They were interrupted by a knock on the door followed by Mr. Kamel ushering in his chadur-covered wife carrying a tray of tea things, oranges, and Minoo hard candies.

"I will make my wife not disturb you," said Mr. Kamel as he shooed her before him out of the room and shut the door.

"Mendacious bastard," muttered Groves after the door had shut. "I'm sure he woke his wife up to make us this tea. She always goes to bed right after preparing our dinner. By the way, if you feel like it, you might think of taking your dinners here. It would save me from talking to Mr. Kamel. Now what were we saying? Oh yes, my class. No, I don't recall you having been in it; but that's all right, I forget most of my students. You said you were coming out to talk to me about an official matter. What would you like to know?"

From experience long past Frank Quintana knew what to expect from Benjamin Groves and was not put off by his abrasiveness. "I'm looking for information that might help clear up a problem we have at the embassy. You may not know that the man who drove you out here to Nishapur died in a car crash about a month and a half ago. His name was Freddy Desuze."

"I'm sorry to hear that," said Groves. "He talked an awful lot, but I liked him. We were together for about three days. Iranian drivers, though, are insane. Still, it's a little surprising. Freddy drove very well."

"It was in the mountains. From all appearances his car was sideswiped around a hairpin curve and pushed into a canyon."

"Happens all the time," Groves said.

"There is just one thing that has raised a problem—a question, actually—about the accident. When the car was recovered, Freddy's short-wave radio was missing. Of course, he could have taken it out of the car, or a thief could have reached the accident first and stolen it, but Ambassador Dermott wanted me to check up on it." Groves was now eying him curiously. "Since you are the last person known to have ridden in his car—with the exception of a woman from the Iran-America Society who was in it at night and can't remember seeing the radio—I thought I should check with you about it."

The rawboned professor half lowered his eyelids and pursed his lips as if he were bargaining with a bazaar merchant. "You drove out here? How long did it take you? Three days?"

"Five," admitted Frank with embarrassment. "I broke down in Damghan, and I got lost in Tehran the day I left."

"Five days here and three days at least going back: eight days. Obviously you expect me to say that the radio was in the car when Desuze drove me out here. Then other questions follow from that. Right? Otherwise you're wasting an awful lot of time."

"*Was* the radio in the car when you came out?"

"Yes, it was, and playing every minute. Fanciest portable outfit I've ever seen. And now I'm going to save you some time." Frank was all attention. "I think I know where that radio is now."

Shock registered on Frank's face. "Where?"

"In the room the mullas take their tea breaks in at the Mohammad Mahruq shrine."

"Where?" said Frank again in an incredulous tone of voice.

"Where what? The Mohammad Mahruq shrine? It's a couple

124

of kilometers east of town on the edge of the ruins. Beautiful. Seventeenth-century tilework."

"I was just there a couple of hours ago," said Frank in confusion.

"Then why did you ask where it is?"

"What's the radio doing *there?* Are you sure it's the same one?"

"No, of course I'm not sure. His name wasn't painted on it. But the damn thing played in my ears for three days, and I remember distinctly what it looked like. The one at the shrine is either the same one or the same exact model, and I've never seen anything like it before in Iran. As for how it got there, I have no idea. Where did you say the accident took place?"

"On the Ab-i Ali road."

"Long, long way from here," said Groves.

"The Mohammad Mahruq shrine, Professor Groves, does it have any relation to the Hossein Makfuf shrine?"

Groves snorted. "Of course it does. Son-of-a-bitch who runs it thinks he owns Hossein Makfuf. He tried to bar me from visiting the place, but I called his bluff. I went out there yesterday and nobody dared to stop me."

"But what exactly is the connection between the two?"

"That's just what I'd like to know! They've built a path from Mohammad Mahruq to the Hossein Makfuf prayer grounds, and there's going to be a procession down that path during the Moharram ceremonies. The mullas will be using Mohammad Mahruq as their base of operations. It has all the room and facilities they need. Hossein Makfuf is just a dinky little place, you know. But, beyond that, I don't know that there's any real connection. I checked the legal status of the land around Hossein Makfuf in Tehran before coming out here. That whole section of ruins was attached as farmland to two villages that used to be owned by a single family. After land reform, the land was sold to the villagers. Then last year that part of the land occupied by the shrine and the prayer grounds was purchased by the Nishapur municipality, apparently on the advice of the

Chief of Education, and transferred to the Religious Endowments Authority. Have you met the chief, Mr. Borumand? You have. Okay. According to Borumand, he got the municipality to purchase the land because he was afraid that the cult that was beginning to spring up would lead to some profiteer's buying the land as a speculation. The funny part, however, is that the Ministry of Culture and Art has never ruled on the genuineness of the tombstone, and Borumand ran a huge risk by anticipating what decision might be reached. Of course, now Hormozi himself is going to come out here and pronounce the Shah's blessing, so Borumand guessed right. He's not the sort to take risks, though." Groves stifled Quintana's attempted interruption with a raised hand. "Just one more thing. The other day Borumand tried to tell me that the mullas at Mohammad Mahruq had jurisdiction over Hossein Makfuf. But he knew perfectly well that was a lie. They may have the right to appoint the custodian of the shrine, because that's purely a religious matter, but they don't have jurisdiction over the land around it. Now, what did you want to say?"

"You mentioned Hormozi. Is that Dr. Mohammad Hormozi, the Minister of Culture and Art?"

"None other. Do you know the bastard?"

"No. What is it exactly that he's going to do here? I didn't quite understand."

"This is supposed to be a big secret, but what I heard is that he's coming here for the Moharram ceremonies and that he's going to announce officially the government's decision that the tomb of Hossein Makfuf is genuine. Then, of course, thirty thousand pilgrims will howl with delight and consider him some sort of saint. It's just the kind of stagy opportunism that he goes for."

Frank Quintana was suddenly looking very serious. "It may be something even worse, Professor Groves. There are some things I think I should tell you."

126

The gemlike blue study of Ayatollah Shirazi in the shrine mosque of Fatima in the holy city of Qom held three men seated on mats: the venerable, white-bearded mulla himself and his two visitors, Ayatollah Pirzadeh and Colonel Ziya. The old man's querulous voice characterized the tone of the meeting.

"You should never have involved Hormozi," he was complaining. "You underestimated him."

The colonel, at whom the criticism was directed, sat cross-legged with a ramrod-straight back, his eyes directed straight ahead as if he were receiving a dressing down from a superior officer. He recollected earlier days when Ayatollah Shirazi had felt the involvement of the minister to be necessary. When he was sure the old man's tirade was finished, he replied firmly, "It was necessary. All of our plans could have been destroyed if the minister had declared the tombstone a fraud. I did not know that he would interest himself in the Twelfth Imam. My intention was simply to impress upon him the seriousness of the matter."

"How much do you think he knows," said Ayatollah Pirzadeh in a calming voice.

"I think he knows nothing important. He has only guesses. He has no means of investigating anything. In any event, he is my responsibility. That is not why we are having this meeting."

"I don't want that hypocrite to speak at the ceremonies," croaked the old man.

"It can't be helped," said Pirzadeh quietly. "Colonel Ziya is right. We have other matters to decide. We must decide about the Americans."

"You said that that man Borumand would prevent the American from interfering. Why didn't he?"

"Mr. Borumand was weak." Pirzadeh was deferential to the white-bearded mulla. "We have removed him."

"The Chief of Police will temporarily serve as Chief of Education in Nishapur," said Colonel Ziya as if to explain Pirzadeh's short statement. "We will keep the Americans—there are now two of them—under surveillance; but it will be difficult to expel them from the city. The older one, Professor Groves, is a hard man to deal with; and the younger one is on the American embassy staff. We don't want to draw attention unnecessarily to Nishapur at this moment."

"I think we should kill them," said Ayatollah Shirazi coldly.

"Out of the question," responded the colonel emphatically.

"The Shah would never forgive us for offending the Americans," added Pirzadeh.

"You're cowards," rasped the old man. "They could disappear the same way the other American disappeared."

Pirzadeh looked embarrassed. "I think we made a mistake in judgment. We acted too hastily in killing him." The other two men looked at him. "We did not anticipate that the car would be recovered after going off the Ab-i Ali road, and my men removed something I thought would prove useful from the car before destroying it. Because of that mistake, the Americans

128

have probably guessed that it was not an accident."

"What was removed that was so valuable to us?" asked Ayatollah Shirazi.

"Just a radio. It was an excellent short-wave radio. I thought we should have such a thing in Nishapur to listen to the calls of the gendarmerie."

"That was very foolish," said Colonel Ziya. "If you had asked, I could have provided a radio."

"It is done," replied Pirzadeh. "But the radio is in a place where it will not be found."

"The Americans will investigate," persisted the colonel.

"Possibly, but they will find nothing."

"We should kill the Americans in Nishapur," croaked Shirazi, returning to his previous position. "Your mistake makes it imperative. They are probably agents of the CIA."

"No," said Colonel Ziya. "I have checked their backgrounds. The one named Groves is a university professor who has been well known in Iran for many years. The other is a young officer in the diplomatic service. He has served in Iran before, but there is no reason to connect him with the CIA. Why he is staying in Nishapur I don't know, but Professor Groves's reason for being there is unquestionably legitimate. To make them disappear would jeopardize all of our plans."

"I agree," said Pirzadeh.

"They are a danger to us," persisted the malevolent old man.

"If they do become a danger, they will be dealt with in the proper manner," said Pirzadeh.

Bending over a snooker table in a large basement room that served as Tehran's only public billiard parlor were an Iranian and an American. From opposite sides of the table they were attempting to judge whether a red ball was completely blocking the path between the cue ball and the yellow ball that it had to come in contact with.

"You're snookered," said the clean-cut, chestnut-haired American, whose name was David Bass.

"Around the corner," replied his dapper opponent, straightening up. His shot rebounded from the cushions on either side of a corner pocket and struck the yellow ball from behind, nearly knocking it into the opposite side pocket.

"Where did you learn to shoot?" asked the American admiringly.

"I went to college in Oklahoma," answered Jamshid Ansari.

"Oklahoma?" the American asked, lining up his next shot. "Where did you meet Zhaleh? She went to Berkeley."

"I know. We were members of the same Iranian students' organization. We were both on the national executive committee. I guess you were at Berkeley at the same time she was, weren't you?"

"Yup." He had now run two numbered balls and two red balls. "We were going together when I was drafted out of graduate school. My board had the notion that students who opposed the war should be sent to Vietnam and used as cannon fodder, so I got reclassified and inducted real quick." He missed a combination. "I thought of going to Canada, but I couldn't make up my mind to do it. So off I went."

Jamshid missed his shot. "You haven't seen Zhaleh since then?"

"Oh, sure I have. We just didn't hit it off again the way we had before. She's real political now. I guess you know that. I'll always be in love with her, though. I told her that." He had just sunk the last ball on the table.

"Did Zhaleh indicate in her telegram what she wanted?"

"Not in so many words," answered Bass in a voice full of innuendo. "I thought you were planning to tell me."

"Perhaps we should go for a walk." Jamshid replaced his cue in the rack and collected his camel's hair coat from a chair. The American followed suit. Jamshid paid for the time on the table, since he had been badly defeated.

It was cold outdoors. There had been snow, but it was temporarily gone from the city although it remained heavy in the mountains that rose above the city to the north. Jamshid had thought for a long time about a safe place to discuss the mission he was going to ask David Bass to perform. The billiard parlor had been his first choice, but he had been unable to get a table that was sufficiently removed from other players. They headed now in Jamshid's red Fiat to his second choice, the Iran-America Society.

Normally the hamburger bar at the Iran-America Society was filled with American students of Persian, savoring a rare taste of home, and Iranians enrolled in English courses trying to find someone to practice on. The cold and the early afternoon hour were working in their favor, however. Without difficulty they found a booth with no occupied tables near it.

"They have pretty good hamburgers here," said Bass.

"Can you kill the Shah?" said Jamshid in a low voice.

The American fixed him with hard greenish eyes. "I told Zhaleh that I could."

"Are you willing to?"

"If Zhaleh wants it," he said flatly. "She never forgave me for not going to Canada. I told her I'd do the Shah if she would come back to me."

Jamshid recalled vividly Zhaleh's torment when David had written announcing the offer.

"I assume she said in her telegram that she would come back to you."

David Bass nodded. "She said she would meet me in Beirut." He took another big bite of his hamburger.

"How would you do it?"

"There are lots of ways. I never told Zhaleh why I was able to make my offer. You see, the Shah doesn't trust his own people."

"Many of them are totally loyal," said Jamshid.

"I'm not talking about loyalty. I'm talking about talent. They made me a helicopter mechanic in Nam. I was real good at it. The Shah doesn't trust any Iranians to service his helicopters. They fly them, but we service them. It's done on contract by an American company. I made it through the security clearance

131

because I had such a good record in Nam, and they never found out that I had had an Iranian girlfriend. So here I am. Every time the Shah goes for a ride, he's depending on me and my trusty wrench."

"But you're not the only mechanic. Your work must be checked by someone."

"Sure it is. I learned some tricks in Nam, though, for getting by an inspection. Of course, I'd have to get my hands on the right stuff."

"We can get what you want." Jamshid was thinking of the truckload of armor that had coasted through from the Soviet Union.

"Well, I guess it's just a matter of when and where, then."

"That will be determined within a few weeks. I'll get in touch with you."

David Bass stood up and stuck out his hand. "Thanks for the hamburger. They make them just like back home here." As he walked away, he called back over his shoulder, "Say hi to Zhaleh for me."

CHAPTER **19**

According to protocol, the meeting in the conference room of the State Department's Near East Division was chaired by Eliot Hauser, Assistant Secretary for Near Eastern Affairs, a worn-looking veteran of endless hours of negotiating with Arabs and Israelis and almost equally taxing hours trying to avoid getting stuck with the roast sheep's eyes at banquets given by Arab oil potentates. The most important man in the room, however, was Emmanuel Holachek, the National Security Advisor, who, accompanied by his bespectacled assistant Bill Keller, was making an infrequent appearance at Foggy Bottom. The others in attendance were CIA senior analyst Milton Kaufman and three much more junior State Department officers: Matthew Hall from the Iran desk, Brenda Badarian from the Iraq desk, and Intelligence and Research specialist on the Near East Paul Huddleston. Holachek had been fifteen minutes late to the meeting, but no one present held a sufficiently powerful post to criticize the delay.

"If you're ready, Emmanuel," said Eliot Hauser with a pronounced Boston accent, "I'll make a brief statement to get things going." Holachek nodded. "Our purpose, gentlemen and lady," he nodded toward Brenda Badarian, who suppressed an angry glare, "is to put together what we know or can guess about the situation that seems to be developing in Iran. As you know, Frank Quintana from this division"—Paul Huddleston, Quintana's co-worker in INR, made note of the bureaucratic misidentification—"has provided some information that seems to be quite suggestive. Matthew, do you want to start us out with some background?" Having relinquished the floor, Hauser settled back to listen, not being himself particularly knowledge-able on Iranian matters.

"In the last four months," began the pallid, round-faced desk officer nervously, "which is approximately how long we have been aware of rumors of a coup, nothing out of the ordinary seems to have happened in Iran. The Shah visited Rumania as scheduled and received visits from the heads of state of Spain, Mauritius, and Dubayy." He leafed through a few pages of notes. "The Empress went on a goodwill visit to Pakistan. The Crown Prince visited England. The Shah made a speech telling the U.S. to reduce its oil consumption and control inflation. Meanwhile, inflation in Iran continues at about thirty percent." He timidly looked up at Holachek. "That's a soft figure. They have price controls on a basic shopping basket of goods which makes it difficult to measure real inflation."

"Is that all?" asked Holachek curtly.

"No, Sir."

"What do you have to say that's germane to what we're here for?"

Matthew Hall looked again at his notes. "Just that nothing has happened that shows any awareness of a coup being planned," he said in a hesitant voice. "No sign of special precautions, no . . ."

"Anything special from Iraq?" asked Holachek brusquely, turning his face to Brenda Badarian.

134

"No, Sir," she said.

"Good. Now, Kaufman, tell us what CIA knows about this fellow Hormozi, who Quintana says might be our Twelfth Imam."

"He looks like a sweetheart. Born in Tehran, forty-two, Minister of Culture and Art for the last three years, before that a university chancellor. His higher education was over here: Caltech in physics and then Yale graduate school in philosophy; did a Ph.D. dissertation, which was later published, on the philosopher Avicenna. He has a reputation among scholars of being a bridge between modern Western culture and traditional Islamic culture. He's published four books in English, one of them a tract on mysticism in the modern world that has sold very well on college campuses. In Iran he has a mixed reputation as a religious leader. Purists and traditionalists find his work shaky, but it goes down well with young people. He's sort of a guru on a minor level. Politically, he's ambitious but apparently pro-West all the way. Absolutely clean record is the word we get through SAVAK. That's about all. Oh. Likes foreign blondes, either in series or in parallel."

"Deep down, not essentially a politician," summarized Holachek.

"Ambitious, but not essentially a politician," replied Kaufman.

"What else do we have that we didn't have before?"

"Sir," said Brenda Badarian, getting the Security Advisor's attention, "the handbills being posted in Iran were printed in Iraq. The paper is the same as that used by the Ba'th Party, but the typeface is the same as that used by the religious authorities in Kerbela to print religious tracts. An Iraqi source says that bunches of handbills have been found in the possession of Iranian pilgrims returning to Iran from visits to Kerbela. That seems to be how they're getting into Iran."

"How do you account for the government paper?" asked Bill Keller.

"It could easily have been stolen. That's more likely than official collaboration. The government has a record of poor relations with the mullas in Kerbela."

"I have something on the mysterious Colonel Ziya," interjected Paul Huddleston from INR, seeing that Brenda Badarian had nothing more to add. "He took a short course in the U.S. at Army Staff College in 1964. He was older than the other Iranians who went through with him, and someone dropped a note in the file suggesting that he was with the group as a kind of political commissar. We also have an old list in the files from 1969 that includes him with a question mark as a member of the SAVAK Inspectorate."

"That's not what we have," put in Milton Kaufman. "We have him still in the army until 1970 and then moving over to SAVAK in a reorganization of the top brass."

"What about personal details?" Holachek asked.

"Just that he's an old-guard loyalist: pro-West, conservative," responded Kaufman.

Huddleston scanned a page of biographical data. "Nothing here to speak of," he said slowly. "He's an Azerbaijani Turk, but that's standard for Iranian officers. Before the army he studied at the Ja'fari Muslim Law College in Qom." Matthew Hall tentatively raised his hand. "Hmmm, wife and four children, oldest son named after the Shah—that's the father of the present Shah. That's about all."

"Do you have something to add, Mr. Hall?" said Bill Keller.

"Yes, Sir. I believe that in 1973 the rector of the Ja'fari Muslim Law College in Qom set off some street demonstrations by complaining about the Shah's refusal to set up a committee of mullas to pass on new laws. His name, as I recall, is Pirzadeh, Ayatollah Pirzadeh. Ayatollah is a religious title."

"What is the committee of mullas all about?" asked Keller.

"It's provided for in the 1907 constitution, but it has never been put into effect. It gives the mullas veto power over laws they think are contrary to Islam."

Holachek intervened. "How old is Pirzadeh?"

136

"Middle-aged, I think," Hall said.

"Then he must have taken over that law college at least twenty years after Colonel Ziya left it. Is that right?"

"Longer, I think, Sir," murmured Hall.

Holachek looked exasperated. "Bill, sum up what we have."

Keller was well known for taking in information rapidly and making coherent sense out of it. "Not very much. From reports that the Twelfth Imam propaganda is proliferating, apparently distributed from the religious centers in Iraq, it seems likely that an effort is being made at destabilization. But this doesn't necessarily mean a coup. It could simply be an effort to impress the Shah with the hold of religion on the masses in order to get him to back off on religious restrictions. If there is a coup in the works, Colonel Ziya seems an unlikely ally of Mohammad Hormozi. If a loyalist like Ziya were going to sell the Shah out, you would expect him to do it in favor of a conservative rather than a modernist."

"What about Hormozi as a figurehead for religious conservatives put up to make a new regime acceptable to the United States?" suggested Holachek.

"Possible," said Keller. "I don't get the impression of Hormozi being anyone's figurehead, but it's possible."

"Okay, that's all," said Holachek abruptly. "Thank you all for coming." The faces around the table looked startled by the suddenness of the dismissal.

Eliot Hauser straightened up in his chair at the head of the table. "Yes, I think we've had a very useful discussion and exchange of views. Thank you, Emmanuel, for coming over and talking with us. Thank you, gentlemen and lady, for your helpful contributions. The meeting is adjourned."

Keller and Holachek elected to walk back to their offices under a bright blue winter sky that had only that day brought to an end a week of low gray clouds. The air was brisk and, by Washington standards, cold, but they walked rather slowly in order to continue a conversation begun as they left the building.

"So you think that it *is* a coup," said Keller, observing his superior's look of serious concern.

"I didn't say that. I only said that if it is one, its pattern is one that normal counter-measures are not designed to handle. Instead of using the army or gendarmerie to stage the coup, the idea seems to be to immobilize them with religion or win part of them over after the coup takes place. I wonder if that's feasible in Iran."

"It's not my specialty, but I've heard Milton Kaufman and Frank Quintana say over and over that, despite all the oil money, Iran is far more underdeveloped than Turkey or most of the Arab countries. For comparison you might think back to the Imam of Yemen in the sixties. He was a religious ruler from a brand of Islam similar to the Iranian one, and he was able to carry on a civil war for years against Egyptian troops. I wouldn't want to underestimate the power of Iranian religion even among the younger, Westernized people."

"You're thinking of the Islamic Marxists?"

Keller nodded. "Kaufman didn't mention them today, but earlier on he thought they were involved."

"Supposing a coup works and this fellow Hormozi ends up on top as a real leader or as a front man, what happens then?"

"I don't know. I imagine he would use his religious position to promulgate a new constitution more favorable to Islam. Probably reverse some of the reforms of the last twenty years."

"But beyond that?"

Keller thought for a minute. "Are you thinking of Saudi Arabia?"

"Mm-hmmm."

"If a puritanical, conservative Muslim regime in an Arab country can block Russian influence and support American policy, a puritanical, conservative Muslim regime in Iran can do the same. Is that it? From an American point of view, Hormozi as the Twelfth Imam might be as good as the Shah."

"Might even be better," mused Holachek. "The roots of the Shah's popularity aren't very secure, and dynastic succession is a real risk. Didn't you say that Iran specialists doubt that his son will ever make it to power?"

"Some do. It depends on how old he is when his father dies. A minority with the Empress as regent isn't very promising."

"But, with a pro-American Twelfth Imam fifteen years younger than the Shah, the succession problem could be put off for an additional decade or two, and there would be alternatives to the dynastic model when the succession did come."

"Are you thinking that it wouldn't be so bad for the United States if the Shah went down?"

"Nope. I'm just thinking that that's something we should begin to think about. This whole business may be leading nowhere; but if it does go toward a coup, we may have to make some very quick decisions. I want us to be ready for them."

The two men walked on for a block without saying anything more. Then Holachek seemed to have made up his mind.

"Bill, I know you don't have very much work to do." The young man smiled ruefully. "I want you to work up a background paper for a possible presidential decision memorandum. Don't tell anyone what it's about. There are a lot of alarmists around. Cover the likely ramifications of a change to a conservative religious government in Iran: trade, oil prices, armaments, Soviet reactions, relations with other Muslim countries, whatever else you think is important. If anyone gives you trouble on releasing information, have him call me. You got that?"

"When do you want it?"

"Can you do it in two weeks?"

"I can do it better in three."

"Three then. But if a coup comes in two, you're fired."

Dhu al-Hijja: The Fifth Month

CHAPTER 20

"It is better to say in English 'strangled' or 'throttled'?" inquired Mr. Kamel of the two stunned-looking Americans seated at his dining table. He fit his hands around his neck to illustrate what he meant.

"You mean the Chief of Education has been strangled?"

"It is strangled, then?"

"Yes, the right word is 'strangled,'" answered Ben Groves with unprofessorial impatience. "Now, how do you know this about Mr. Borumand?"

"Wife of my brother has brother who teaches in Sabzavar. Mr. Borumand's body was finded by gendarmes and brought to Sabzavar. Everyone recognized him."

"But the Chief of Police told me that Mr. Borumand had been called to Tehran and that he was in charge until Borumand returned."

Mr. Kamel shrugged his shoulders.

"He evidently didn't get to Tehran," observed Frank Quintana.

"And the police chief has been using his trip as an excuse to keep me from going out to Hossein Makfuf." The heat in Groves's voice showed that he was unaccustomed to being deceived.

"Do you think it's deliberate?"

"A conspiracy? That's your department, not mine. I only know that a small-town police chief is preventing me from doing my work." He glanced at the attentive face of Mr. Kamel. "What do you say we go for a walk in the evening air, Frank?" he added in a suggestive voice.

"Good idea." Quintana rose from the table.

"It is very cold tonight," put in Mr. Kamel plaintively. The Americans had slipped into their shoes and were already headed for the central passageway that opened onto the courtyard.

"Nosy son-of-a-bitch was right," said Groves with a shiver after they had left the courtyard. "Let's get into your car."

The conversation that they had pursued so often during the week Frank Quintana had been staying in Nishapur and taking his dinners at Mr. Kamel's house was resumed in the darkness of the International Scout. As usual, Quintana put the case for there being a conspiracy centered on the cult of Hossein Makfuf, and Groves took a skeptical approach. The latter's interviews with the pilgrims who had begun to move into the tents by the railroad station had convinced him that the devotees of Hossein Makfuf were simple believers from the humbler walks of life. He had noted references in their conversation to the Twelfth Imam, whom some of them expected to reappear during the Moharram ceremonies, but he had come across nothing that fit the image of pre-revolutionary messianic fervor that Frank Quintana talked about. In response, Frank maintained that the movement was one that would come to a head very quickly just before Moharram, since to peak too early would invite government intervention and suppression.

Normally, the professor's fixed opinions led to a deadlock, but Frank persisted because he had decided that Groves and

144

Groves alone had the necessary understanding of the Hossein Makfuf phenomenon to ferret out the truth about Freddy Desuze's fatal involvement. The news of the Chief of Education's inexplicable death for the first time led to a weakening of Groves's skepticism. After half an hour of discussion that quickly heated up the inside of the car, Frank started the engine, switched on the headlights, and pulled away from the curbside ditch.

Except in the vicinity of the central intersection, where two small chelo kebab restaurants were still lighted and the Armenian hotel still purveying drink to sinners, storefronts were dark and the streets nearly deserted. Frank drove on past the turnoff to his hotel and headed out of town on the shadowy, tree-lined road to Mashhad. At the side road to the Omar Khayyam monument and Mohammad Mahruq shrine the car slowed and turned. It passed the chain-blocked road to Hossein Makfuf and proceeded to the point where the paved road climbed the railroad embankment to cross the tracks. There it drove off the right-hand side of the road and came to a stop in the dark pocket formed by the merging of the railroad embankment and the built-up road. Despite the bright moonlight, the dousing of the vehicle's headlights rendered it practically invisible in the shadows.

Frank had pressed for a cross-country approach to the Hossein Makfuf shrine from the north, but Groves had vetoed it on the grounds that treasure hunters' excavations made it too dangerous to attempt even on a bright night. He had also derided Frank's fears that the road or the shrine would be guarded at night, and as they approached the chain blocking the road, his confidence appeared to be justified.

The moonlit landscape of ravaged ruins on either side of the road provided an aura of mystery and unreality as they strolled with forced casualness down the road, but nothing moved. The bark of a jackal provided the only sound. No artificial lights were to be seen, since the city and the Mohammad Mahruq shrine were behind them. Only when the Hossein Makfuf shrine itself came into view, looking eerily white in the moonlight, did a dim spot of yellow light showing through the tiny window in the shrine's dome. Groves knew that his friend the custodian lived in the shrine and soothed Frank's nerves with the information.

Finally, they reached the huge rectangular prayer grounds. Little more than a week had elapsed since Groves had made his last visit in defiance of the deceased Mr. Borumand's wishes, but great changes had taken place. The low reviewing stand for dignitaries on the east side in front of the shrine was noticeably further toward completion, and the area where the closed tent pavilions of the women would go up was clearly being worked on. The most impressive change, however, was the great platform that had sprung up in the center of the rectangle's western side.

From a distance they surveyed the six-meter-high structure and the dark profile of a flatbed truck parked beside it. No guards were in evidence. Without undue haste they approached the platform, which loomed even larger than it had previously looked once they were standing beside it. The space beneath the platform was pitch black, for although the front and sides of the base were open, presumably to be covered with black mourning draperies during Moharram, the back side was a solid wall that prevented them from seeing through to the Mohammad Mahruq shrine in the distance on the far side.

It took a while to find the stairs to mount the structure. They were behind the solid wall at the back. Cautiously Frank and Groves climbed up. The flooring was finished except for two areas at either end that could easily be seen as dark squares. Uprights rising at the back suggested that some sort of overhead construction had yet to be completed, but otherwise there was nothing distinctive about the platform's surface. After a few minutes looking at the ghostly landscape and the soft glow of Nishapur's street lighting in the distance, there was nothing else to do but descend.

Going down into the darkness promised to be a more treacherous undertaking than climbing up had been. Groves clutched one of the uprights for support as his foot explored the depth of the first step. Standing a few paces behind him, Frank leaped forward and grabbed the professor's arm at the sudden cry he uttered as he stepped down.

"What the hell are you doing?" said Groves.

"Keeping you from falling. You cried out."

"I only said 'Hey!' I'm not such a doddery old fool that I can't make it down the steps by myself."

Frank let go of his arm. "Then what did you call 'hey' for?"

"Because I just noticed something. Feel this two by four. Tell me what you think it's made of."

Frank reached out and stroked the vertical beam. "Doesn't feel like wood," he said tentatively. "Doesn't feel like a painted surface either. Sort of a funny texture. It certainly isn't metal. Besides, you wouldn't need such a big beam if you used metal. You'd just use a pipe or something like that."

"It's almost like plastic," said Groves.

"Hardly likely out here in the sticks. What are you doing?"

Groves was busying himself with something on the beam. "Just trying to sliver off a bit with my pocket knife. It doesn't seem to cut. So I guess it's not paint. Feel the floor. Is it the same stuff?"

Frank's shadowy profile bent over the straightened up. "Yup, same stuff."

"Then this whole platform must be made of the building materials that came through on that flatbed truck a couple of weeks ago. I recall seeing it and wondering where it was headed. This is brick and concrete country; you don't see many truckloads of lumber, much less this stuff—whatever it is."

"It can't be very strong," came Frank's voice from a point he had wandered to toward the end of the platform. "This flooring must be four inches thick. It's way more than they need. Let's check downstairs and see how the rest of it's built."

Ten more minutes of feeling their way about produced the information that the supporting beams and back wall of the structure were of comparable dimensions and all of the same material. The supporting beams themselves were well set in concrete. Even the stairway to the top of the platform was of the same sturdy construction.

"It's just not the way things get built in Iran," mused Groves when they had finished their investigation.

"Damn near killed myself going underneath there," said Frank. "They've got a big hole dug in the middle."

"I told you not to go there. Do you have any idea why a load of heavy building material should be trucked in from god knows where to put up a temporary platform for a peasant revival meeting in the middle of nowhere?"

"None at all. Which way was the truck coming from?"

"Tehran."

"That's funny, too. Mashhad is two days closer and has any kind of building stuff you might need."

Neither of them said a word for several minutes. Groves broke the silence. "It's cold. Let's go back."

Without further comment they turned back toward the gravel road. Nothing more was said during the walk. Both men were too absorbed in their own thoughts to appreciate the ghostly beauty of the craggy, moon-swept landscape, or to notice that two sturdy, athletic-looking Iranians in cheap, dark blue suits that made them blend into their shadowy surroundings were seated in a field near the chained-off entrance to the road at a point where they could survey both the road itself and the International Scout parked by the railroad embankment.

CHAPTER **21**

Zhaleh Hekmat had made up her mind. Time was growing short, and she was still entirely in the dark regarding the plans for the Twelfth Imam's reappearance. The shunning she received daily from the mullas at Mohammad Mahruq had been reinforced by a group of stolid, husky young men who had arrived from out of town and taken up residence in the shrine. No one told her who the men were, but the constant watch they kept on people going to the Hossein Makfuf shrine was enough to tell her that they were agents of Ayatollah Pirzadeh. She could not even visit the site where the reappearance would probably take place since she had been explicitly forbidden by the chief mulla from walking over to the smaller shrine and the prayer grounds. With the new contingent of Pirzadeh's men, even to try slipping over with the handfuls of pilgrims that made their way each day to bask in the holiness of the saint's tomb was out of the question. She was too well known to the silent guards, and the pilgrim's ritual of prayer and meditation would give her no opportunity to reconnoiter the area even if she did slip by. Her only alternative was the Americans. Since she had already made a point of avoiding contact with the professor, she settled for the handsome younger man who had arrived only two weeks before.

For an Iranian young woman to meet a foreign young man by accident was a virtual impossibility in Nishapur, and even the number of places where they could talk after such an improbable meeting was severely limited. The two fancier chelo kebab restaurants and the new hotel constituted just about the entire list. As Zhaleh headed purposefully for the new tourist hotel, she wondered how she was going to manage to meet Quintana.

It turned out to be easier than she had thought. He was sitting in the hotel's rudimentary lounge across from the dining room. The television set was on even though he was the only person there to watch it, and he was obviously engrossed in an Agatha Christie mystery. Zhaleh seated herself on the streamlined plastic upholstered armchair nearest him. She arranged her chadur to allow more than the prescribed amount of her head and neck to be seen.

"You are American, aren't you?" she asked in an American accent perfected by four years in graduate school at Berkeley.

Someone else who wanted to practice her English. Frank looked up with a forbidding expression that indicated that he had been deeply involved in his book. The girl looking at him with such a warm smile was simply beautiful. He closed the book in his lap.

"Yes, I'm American," he said in his most cordial tone. "Are you Iranian? You speak English like an American." He knew perfectly well that the chances of there being an American woman wearing a chadur in an obscure city like Nishapur were nil.

"I went to school at Berkeley for four years. I hear American English so seldom out here away from Tehran that I get homesick whenever I do. I heard you talking English with your friend one day in the post office."

Frank couldn't recall visiting the post office with Professor Groves, but he was not about to let the discrepancy worry him. "He's a college professor. I'm with the U.S. embassy in Tehran. My name is Frank Quintana."

"Chicano?"

"No." Frank felt a bit embarrassed. "Actually, my father came to the United States from Spain after Franco won the Civil War."

"How exciting," said Zhaleh. "Was he a loyalist?"

"Yes. He was a socialist. It almost screwed up my clearance when I went into the foreign service."

"I was a radical at Berkeley myself in the 1960s," said Zhaleh proudly.

"Didn't that make it difficult to come back here to Iran?"

"No. My family is too important. Besides, the Shah isn't afraid of female radicals."

"Is your family from Nishapur?"

"No, Tehran. I've been banished here to live with relatives. I'm dying of loneliness. This is the most boring, backward, provincial place in the whole world." Her large dark eyes expressed the pain of her loneliness.

"What were you banished for?" asked Frank, gazing into the dark, lonely eyes.

"An affair of the heart," replied Zhaleh dramatically. For an instant she was fearful that she had been too dramatic, but the American's blush told her that she was reading him correctly.

"Where do you live?" he asked tentatively.

"I can't tell you. My family would disapprove of my meeting a man, especially an American." She could tell that Frank Quintana was already seeing himself as part of an intrigue. "I would like to talk to you again sometime. It's been so long since I've heard anything about the United States. Unfortunately, I must go now."

"Of course you can talk to me again," said Frank enthusiastically. "Any time. Perhaps we could, ah, have dinner someplace." She shook her head sadly. "Well, whatever you suggest will be all right with me."

"I will get in touch with you," she said conspiratorially. "Now I must go." Gracefully she stood up, drew her chadur around her in such a way that it showed the outline of her slender figure, and left the hotel. Once outside she sighed deeply. It depressed her to think that, in the long run, being a radical did not seem to weigh as heavily as being a pretty woman.

"The most incredible thing happened," said Frank Quintana excitedly as soon as he entered Mr. Kamel's reception room for his customary conversation with Professor Groves before dinner.

Groves looked up from a dog-eared sheaf of papers he was holding. "You solved the mystery of Freddy Desuze?"

"No, entirely different. An absolutely gorgeous Iranian girl came up to me in the hotel and started a conversation." Groves looked surprised. "I was surprised, too. That doesn't even happen very often in Tehran, especially with the ones wearing chadurs."

"She was wearing a chadur?" Groves asked.

"Yup. She's been sent out here by her family for some sort of indiscretion in Tehran. She's bored stiff. Went to school at Berkeley. You wouldn't believe her face."

Groves squinted his eyes slightly. "Large, dark eyes, prominent jaw and cheekbones, lean look in the cheeks, straight nose, symmetrical . . ."

"How did you know?" Frank's mouth gaped with wonder.

"I saw her arrive in Nishapur about three months ago. I've seen her a few times since then, but I've never spoken to her. I have a feeling she may be avoiding me. Also, if her family has rusticated her from Tehran, they picked a pretty funny way of doing it. She's supposedly working as a servant in the Mohammad Mahruq shrine."

"But she said . . ."

"And in addition, she didn't arrive here alone. She had a very nicely dressed young man with her."

"A brother?" Frank asked feebly.

"On the other hand, the fact that she speaks English just proves my guess that the story I heard about her being a servant doesn't hold water. I wonder who she is."

Frank brightened. "Perhaps I can find out. She wants to talk to me again." He had an additional thought. "If Freddy Desuze's radio is at Mohammad Mahruq, she might even know something about it. I definitely think I should make it a point to see her again."

Groves smiled wryly. "If you're done justifying what you are intending to do in any case, you might want to hear something exciting I've found out today."

"Go right ahead."

"That little mulla out at Hossein Makfuf told me a long time ago that at the Moharram ceremonies there's going to be a performance of a play about the martyrdom of Hossein Makfuf."

"I thought you told me that no one knows what happened to him."

"No one does, but that doesn't prevent someone making up a play. The passion play about Ali's son that is usually put on during Moharram isn't entirely historical, either. Anyhow, he told me it was all a secret, but I got him to loan me his copy of the script just the same. I was reading it today. The handwriting is ghastly. The interesting part is here near the end. Hossein Makfuf is tortured and executed by evil soldiers who chase him to Nishapur after his father's revolt is put down. After taking a long time dying, he goes up on the platform and prays while a light from heaven shines on him. The text of the prayer is a real tearjerker about his murdered father and his murdered brother and so forth."

Frank Quintana had not been paying full attention. "What's the point?"

"The point is that you've been wondering for two weeks about Hossein Makfuf and the Twelfth Imam. If you want my opinion, the ideal moment to have the Twelfth Imam reappear is at the climax of this play."

Frank was now attentive. "But how would it be done? You can't just get up and announce that you're the Twelfth Imam returned to declare the end of the world. It would also rule out Dr. Hormozi unless he's going to be up on the platform with the guy playing Hossein Makfuf. He surely isn't going to play him himself."

"Hormozi may be the wrong person. The unannounced schedule shows him giving a speech on the day following the play, and the script says that Hossein Makfuf is alone on the platform when he gives his final prayer. If you leave Hormozi aside, though, this play gives an ideal opportunity to try something. The audience would be at a peak of emotion." Frank looked doubtful. "You don't have to agree. The conspiracy theory is yours, not mine. I just thought you might be interested in the play."

There was a timid knock, followed by Mr. Kamel entering the reception room. "My wife has prepared dinner," he announced as he did every night.

While they ate, a blind mulla with a thick, rough staff completed a long day's trek by reaching the city of Sabzavar. He accepted guidance to a humble hostel for poor travelers. The proprietor looked at his radiant face and decided not to charge him for the bed. It would be a three-day walk from Sabzavar to Nishapur.

CHAPTER **22**

Frank Quintana was both excited and depressed when he deciphered a telegram from the embassy. He was excited because it confirmed his suspicions about the beautiful Iranian girl in the chadur, suspicions which had grown ever stronger during the three days since Professor Groves had told him what he knew about her situation in Nishapur. His request to the embassy for a check of university, immigration, FBI, and CIA records had turned up the information that an Iranian woman named Zhaleh Hekmat had indeed taken a degree in electrical engineering at the University of California at Berkeley during the sixties. She had been active in radical Iranian student politics and was tentatively identified as a member of an underground group in Iran known as the Muslim Marxist Alliance. Not only did this confirm his suspicions, but it was welcome reassurance that his protracted stay in Nishapur was not simply a wild-goose chase.

At the same time, he was depressed. A second conversation in the hotel lobby the day before had convinced him that, however involved she might be in some sort of conspiracy, she was also a troubled as well as a beautiful girl. She had told him that he reminded her of her old American boyfriend whom she had loved before he went off to Vietnam. She seemed so sad at thinking about him that Frank had asked whether he had been killed. She had shaken her head and told him that, far from being killed, he was working now in Tehran. Frank had not pursued the matter further since her bitter tone of voice made it evident that her family's intervention to nip the renewed love affair in the bud was the cause of her banishment to Nishapur.

Now, with his scrawled decipherment in hand, he ruefully remembered his delicate consideration of her feelings. He had forgotten during their talk that she was not actually in Nishapur because of family pressures. Hence, the tender story of the separated lovers could only be a fabrication. He marveled at the seemingly genuine emotion she had been able to put into the story, and also at his own naïveté in accepting it so trustingly. The short course the CIA had given him had not included lessons in how to disbelieve a sad and beautiful woman. He tried to recall the name of her pretended American boyfriend, but it wouldn't come back. She had mentioned it just once as if by accident. Even such an apparent slip of the tongue had probably been a planned part of her effort to win his sympathy. But what was her purpose? It seemed unlikely that she knew his reason for being in Nishapur. But it was obvious that she was leading him on for some specific purpose. Frank looked at his watch and sighed. He had an appointment to meet her in half an hour. Regretfully he resolved to be really on his guard this time.

The instructions on how to get to the servant's house where Zhaleh had asked him to meet her were not entirely clear to a newcomer to Nishapur. At the entrance to the bazaar, Frank stopped to consider whether she had meant the north or south segment when she had told him to go through the bazaar and out the far end. As he looked across the wide thoroughfare, one of the long-distance buses arriving from Mashhad cut his line of sight. Blazoned on its side were the initials of the bus company in both Persian and Latin characters. The Latin initials caught his eye: B.A.S. A dangling thread of memory suddenly wove itself into place. The letters were almost the name of Zhaleh's boyfriend. She had called him David Bass. The memory was now so vivid he could almost hear her say the name and then suddenly change the subject.

When Frank finally reached the humble house off the alley behind the bazaar, he was ten minutes late. It had taken him that long to go to the post office and send a cryptically worded telegram to Tehran.

Zhaleh was waiting for him in the house. She had bought a few things to make the poor main room of the house that Jamshid had rented look a bit richer and better furnished, but she had been worried that the handsome American would not appear.

The question became moot as his figure appeared in the open doorway. She beckoned him to the cushions on the opposite side of the newly purchased bronze tray she had put in the center of the room.

"I will get us some tea," she said. She rose and left the room. Frank had only a few moments to look around at the room's furnishings. "This house is where one of my uncle's servants lives," she explained as she reappeared with the almost ritual tea, oranges, and Minoo hard candies. "I bribed her so that we might have some privacy." Her voice was light and chatty.

The conversation took a much less emotional direction than it had the day before, and Frank thought that she was as beautiful when she laughed as when she looked sad. It was with an effort that he kept his suspicions high.

After a while she said, "You know, you haven't asked me why I wear a chadur. I usually get asked that because most women who study abroad abandon it as too conservative and old-fashioned."

"I just figured it was because you were here in Nishapur. This is a pretty conservative part of the country. The kids might throw stones at you if you went without it."

157

"Actually, I wear it in Tehran, too, though I never wore it as a little girl. I only began after I came back from the United States." She gave him a little smile that teased him to ask more.

Suddenly Frank recalled some of the clandestine propaganda he had read put out by students calling themselves Islamic Marxists. "It's not really such a bad custom," he began tentatively. He saw that his comment had surprised her. "Of course, I'm not a Muslim, and I know it's a rule that conservative Muslims insist on. But one might ask oneself who contributes more to Iranian society: the typical Westernized, bourgeois woman of Tehran, who has her hair done four times a week and is expected to spend her time flirting with men at parties, or a modest woman who wears a chadur and goes about her business, whether as a traditional woman or a modern woman?"

"I've never heard any American say that," said Zhaleh with undisguised approval in her voice.

Frank felt he was pursuing the right track. "Iranian men aren't ready yet for liberated women. What they want are pretty ornaments with low necklines to show off to their Westernized friends. Until the time comes when they are ready to treat women as human beings, it might be just as well to continue wearing the chadur."

"But don't you find it unattractive?" asked Zhaleh. "Most American men feel that it covers up too much."

Frank laughed. "In that respect, I might agree, but I was brought up in the United States not in Iran."

Zhaleh smiled. "Let me take these tea things away."

It took her longer to dispose of the cups and orange rinds than it had to fetch them. Frank was beginning to wonder what had become of her when she reappeared.

"I'm sorry I took so long. What were we talking about? Oh yes, the chadur. You were saying you didn't find it sexy."

She looked like a beautiful shrouded statue standing just inside the door. "I don't think I said that exactly," began Frank.

"Nor should you," cut in Zhaleh. With a single, confident

motion she drew apart both sides of the dark blue shroud. Beneath it she was totally naked.

Frank's mouth went suddenly dry. He stared at her heavy, dark-nippled breasts and dense black triangle of hair, then he rose to meet her as she walked toward him. She spread out the thin blue garment to either side like a ceremonial robe. It provided stark contrast for her slender white body. Frank gathered her in his arms and drew her down onto the cushions.

They made love in a silent frenzy. Weeks of monastic abstinence in the puritanical environment of Nishapur were released on both sides. Neither plots nor suspicions distracted either of them from taking complete pleasure in the other's body.

In the post-climactic peace their minds returned to previous considerations. They talked of little things and murmured sweet words, but both of them were trying to think through what had happened. Zhaleh was the first to come to a decision.

"Frank?"

"Ummm?"

"I loved it, Frank." She hesitated. "But I did it because I wanted you to do something for me."

"So I guessed."

"I don't want you to ask me why or ask me to explain some of the untrue things I've told you. I just want your help. I need it. It could mean my life."

"I'm not going to murder your father for spoiling your romance," said Frank in an attempt at levity. "It would hardly serve my interest. Short of that, anything's possible."

"Do you promise you won't ask me why? It wouldn't make any difference, anyway, because I wouldn't tell you."

"In that case, just tell me what you want."

"I need to know exactly what is planned for the Moharram ceremonies at Hossein Makfuf. I don't know how you can find out, but I assume your friend Professor Groves can do it. I need to know the complete schedule, where different events are going to take place, everything you can find out."

"Why can't you do it yourself?" asked Frank.

"No questions?"

"No questions," he agreed. "I can find out as much as Groves knows by tomorrow. After that you might be able to be more specific about what you want to know."

For a time neither of them said anything.

Then Zhaleh raised herself on an elbow and laid the top part of her body across his chest. "No matter what, Frank, I'll want to see you again," she whispered softly.

Frank reached for her, and she slid the rest of her body on top of him.

CHAPTER **23**

A daily routine had set in for Benjamin Groves. Mornings he spent studying the organizational and logistical side of the pilgrimage. This meant interviews with various city officials and with the Mashhad merchants who had contracted for seeing to the pilgrims' needs, visits to the now-burgeoning tent site near the railroad station and to the less well-developed location east of town where the pilgrims would be fed from a great open-air kitchen, and occasional talks with an officer of the Nishapur branch of the Iranian National Bank, whom Groves had cultivated as a potential source of information on the financial aspects of the enterprise. He deeply regretted that his relations with the religious authorities had deteriorated to the point that the mullas refused to speak to him, but he was partially consoled by the lunches he was able to have from time to time with the custodian of the Hossein Makfuf shrine. For reasons he could not determine, the enthusiastic little mulla acted as though he were unaware that Groves was persona non grata with his superiors in the Mohammad Mahruq shrine.

In the afternoons, Groves would meet the daily train from Tehran and take a tally of the arriving pilgrims. He had made arrangements with clerks at the three long-distance bus company offices to make similar tallies of pilgrims arriving on their various buses, but by now the bulk of the crowd was coming in by rail. A special pilgrimage fare instituted to compete with the bus lines had had considerable impact. In any case, the preponderance of the pilgrims arriving by bus had to make their way to the railroad station tent site eventually because the city's few alternative places to stay had long been filled.

After tallying the crowd, Groves would select people for interviews. He tried to equalize his sample by sex, age, and apparent social condition, but he admitted to himself that he had not been very successful. Younger women would generally not speak to him, and he was frequently unable to determine the social backgrounds of the older women in their uniform black chadurs. By and large, the crowd was a bit younger than he had expected and predominantly from the traditional lower middle class of artisans and small shopowners. Many of the latter had brought goods with them for sale to the other pilgrims, and the tent site was rapidly developing an open-air bazaar of its own. Groves anticipated that a final surge of pilgrims would arrive from nearby towns and villages just a day or two before the ceremonies began. This would appreciably alter the social balance of the throng.

The tapes of his interviews, which he replayed and translated for his field notes every evening after his usual dinner with Frank Quintana, revealed a broad spectrum of religious motivations among the pilgrims. The ill were seeking cures, the disturbed were seeking solace, and a large number testified to making the pilgrimage in fulfillment of a vow of one sort or another. All of this he had expected. The unexpected was the high percentage who, under prolonged questioning, eventually admitted that they believed that the Twelfth Imam was destined to reappear at the ceremonies. Groves tried to pin down the source of the belief, but inevitably the path led into a maze of rumor and hearsay. The only clear distinction he could make was between those who believed that Hossein Makfuf would himself return as the Twelfth Imam and those who believed that the manifest holiness of Hossein Makfuf would invite the Twelfth Imam to return. It was taken for granted by everyone that the discovery of the tomb of the blind saint had been a divine miracle, and Groves carefully refrained from saying that it was he who had discovered the tombstone and made its existence known, and that he was conscious of no divine influence over his actions. He wondered whether in ten years' time all knowledge of his crucial contribution to the birth of the cult would have been suppressed in favor of the hand of God reaching out to touch and alter the affairs of man.

Ever since his nighttime visit to the prayer grounds with Frank Quintana, Groves had been aware that he was being watched during his afternoon interviews with the pilgrims. It was not always the same person, but the type never varied. His watchers were all stocky, muscular young men dressed like workers but clearly not peasants. Groves guessed that they had been assigned to him by the mullas to see that he did not create a religious disturbance of some kind, but he was not truly satisfied with his own guess. Perhaps they were just supposed to make him feel unwanted. But, if that was their mission, Groves had no trouble resisting the pressure. He didn't care whether he was wanted or not as long as his work was not interfered with.

The mullas themselves rarely appeared among the tents by the railroad station, so the arrival of one whom Groves had never seen before was a noteworthy event. The new arrival was walking slowly down the middle of the broad street that connected the main intersection with the railroad station. Around him was a cluster of a dozen adults and the usual handful of children that gathered whenever anything of interest took place. The customary white turban and brown robe were supplemented by a thick, roughly finished staff with which the

163

mulla carefully measured his steps. As the unexpected figure drew closer, Groves suddenly realized that he was blind. It was not his slow but confident pace that revealed the fact so much as the cant of his head lifted above the ordinary line of sight as if directing his gaze toward an unseen object on the horizon.

Inexplicably, a crowd began to gather at the point where the mulla would enter the tent site. Groves too drifted in that direction, straining to pick up any conversation that might tell him who the newcomer was. All he heard was voice after voice murmuring that the mulla was blind. Only slowly did the repetition of the statement awaken in his mind the realization of its possible significance. Impatiently, he began to insinuate his way to the front of the crowd, determined to test the astounding idea that had just occurred to him.

By the time the blind mulla had entered the tent site, Groves was near the front row of onlookers. Respectfully the crowd gave way before the mulla's stately approach. Groves heard murmured prayers and pious exclamations in his vicinity. He stood his ground as people pressed backward on either side of him until he was almost directly in the mulla's path. Knowing that within moments he would be pushed or pulled out of the way, Groves asked his vital question in a clear, loud voice.

"Are you Hossein Makfuf?"

The mulla halted. His sightless but nevertheless seemingly piercing eyes turned directly toward Groves. "If God wills, I am," he replied serenely. A chorus of pious ejaculations rose in response. Groves drew a breath.

"Are you the Hidden Imam?"

The same serene voice responded without hesitation. "If God wills."

At that moment the stocky young man who had been watching Groves all afternoon shouldered his way out of the crowd and spoke into the mulla's ear. Instantly, the blind holy man resumed his forward pace. Groves continued to hear prayers being murmured as now other people stepped into the mulla's path to try to touch him or kiss his hand. Quickly, a group of men formed themselves into a moving shield to protect the mulla's progress. At the same time, Groves heard the first mutterings of discontent at the effrontery of the unbelieving Christian who had accosted him.

With a studiously relaxed but rapid pace Groves made for the main street, down which the mulla had come a few minutes before. The crowd parted for him, but he could see an increasing number of angry faces. Before a genuine mob atmosphere could develop, however, he had reached the main street and was heading for the center of town.

Absorbed in his work, Groves didn't notice that Frank Quintana was unusually late for dinner. Only when Mr. Kamel tapped on his bedroom door and poked his head in to ask him whether Mr. Quintana was coming to eat the dinner his wife had prepared did the lanky professor notice the hour. At the same moment, however, there was a buzz at the courtyard door.

"I'd almost given you up for lost," observed Groves as he led Quintana into the bleak reception room for their usual preprandial conversation. Mr. Kamel's appealing look told him that dinner was already prepared, but he wanted to inform Frank in private of his most recent discovery.

Frank Quintana had a difficult time showing enthusiasm, but he freely acknowledged that Groves's identification of the person who expected to be chosen by God in the next two weeks to usher in the end of the world was an extraordinary accomplishment.

"I've been studying the play about Hossein Makfuf from the point of view of its climaxing in the revelation of the Twelfth Imam. It fits beautifully. It's really a very skillfully written drama. I could almost believe that Hormozi himself wrote it."

Frank looked at him with mild curiosity. "What's Dr. Hormozi got to do with it? I thought you didn't buy my conspiracy theory. Have you changed your mind?"

"Isn't it obvious?" replied Groves with surprise. "After all, that blind mulla I talked to may believe he's Hossein Makfuf, but he can't be the Twelfth Imam."

Frank looked blank.

"If you had paid attention in my course, you would know that the Twelfth Imam must be perfect in mind and body. No blind man would ever be accepted by the mullas."

"But I thought you said . . ."

"I said he *expects* to be the Twelfth Imam because he obviously expects God to give him back his sight and transform him. In other words, he's a nut. But whoever has been getting propaganda printed up in Iraq obviously isn't going to count on divine intervention. Therefore, the blind man goes into the play as Hossein Makfuf, and someone else is revealed to be the Twelfth Imam. Some of the pilgrims even say they are expecting this, that Hossein Makfuf will 'invite' God to send the Messiah. Now this is very hypocritical planning on the part of the person who dreamed it up. I really can't believe the mullas themselves would sink so low. It's the most callous sort of manipulation of religious feeling. There's only one other alternative: Dr. Mohammad Hormozi. I don't know how he's fooled people into helping him pull it off—possibly they don't even know what he's planning to do—but there's no doubt in my mind that he's going to try to become recognized as the Twelfth Imam right here in Nishapur at the start of Moharram. I've even got the hypothesis written into my field notes with today's date—with due acknowledgment to you for helping me figure it out, of course."

Frank looked startled. "It's in your field notes?"

"Yes, but there's nothing to worry about. I won't publish anything until it happens, anyway. If you want, I can drop out your name for publication and just say 'an American official.' "

"Is the possible overthrow of the Iranian government nothing to you but material for another academic article in some obscure journal?" Frank's voice was a mixture of anger and incredulity.

"I can hardly stretch it into a book," replied Groves sarcastically. "If you don't like what's going to happen and want to try to stop it, that's your business. By the way, how did your meeting with little Miss Scheherazade come off?"

The emotion immediately disappeared from the young man's face. "It was all right," he said vaguely.

"Why did she want to meet you in private?"

"In private? Oh. She had a favor she wanted to ask me to do. Some, uh, things to give to someone back in Tehran. She didn't want to hand them to me in public."

Groves was eying him curiously. "I thought you were going to wire the embassy and find out more about her. You don't sound as suspicious of her as you did a couple of days ago. Did they give her a clean bill of health?"

"They haven't answered yet," Frank lied.

Mr. Kamel's familiar tap sounded at the door.

CHAPTER 24

Ayatollah Pirzadeh placed an irregular lump of hard sugar between his teeth and his cheek and sucked his tea through it. The
teacup was of antique blue porcelain with gold decoration; it
harmonized with the brightly painted, mirror-studded walls of
the small mosque he had chosen for a brief meeting with Colonel Ziya. While drinking tea, the two men were strolling together along an arched corridor flooded with a clear winter
light from windows recently built to fill in the open arches.

"I have given orders for the two Americans to be taken prisoner," said the dark-visaged mulla.

"It is not a good idea," replied the colonel more as an observation than as a criticism.

"I waited as long as possible. Ayatollah Shirazi was pressing
to have them killed, and he is not without power in Nishapur.
They had to be captured for their own safety. Shirazi is becoming obsessed with them."

The colonel nodded and stroked his fine white mustaches.
"The American embassy will make inquiries, of course."

"That is why I felt I must tell you immediately. You must find a way to forestall them. It will be for only two weeks. They can be released after it is over."

"Will they know too much by then?"

"I think not. My men who will guard them in Nishapur are entirely loyal and will tell them nothing. When they are released, they will know only what they know now, but nothing more."

"And what do they know now?"

Pirzadeh laughed. "That I do not know. We have tried to keep them away from the prayer grounds without using force, but we have not been entirely successful. They have seen the platform and climbed on it—but only in the dark. The professor, in particular, does not intimidate easily. Our attempts to keep him from questioning the pilgrims have not succeeded. He even confronted the blind one and asked him directly if he was Hossein Makfuf and the Twelfth Imam."

The colonel stopped walking and turned in alarm to look at the mulla. "Then he must know! How else could he ask such questions?"

Pirzadeh placed his teacup on a carved wooden windowsill. "Clearly he knows what the pilgrims tell him they are expecting to happen. It was luck that brought the blind man to him. But I do not think he understands the political implications of what he knows, and I am sure that he does not know in detail what is going to happen."

"How can you be sure? Who else does he speak to? Perhaps the other American, the diplomat, is more wise politically."

"That is possible. In fact, that is quite likely. We still do not know why the young one is staying so long in Nishapur. As for the professor, the only person he contacts who is not one of us is the custodian from the Hossein Makfuf shrine, our sacrificial lamb. Unfortunately, we dare not involve him in our plans because he must appear to be in league with the Communists when all is done. But, by the same token, there is nothing that he can tell the professor that could damage us."

"And the other American? Who does he see?"

"No one but the professor. Otherwise, he has met only with the Communist woman who is staying at the shrine." The colonel lifted his eyebrows. "They were followed to a small house, but all they did was fornicate like animals." The disgust was heavy in the mulla's voice. "It is typical, Colonel, of what happens to our women who study abroad. Even when they put on the chadur and pretend to be modest, they are no better than whores."

"But could the woman have told him anything during their . . . mmm . . ."

Pirzadeh smiled. "If you are asking whether my men were hiding under the bed, Colonel, the answer is no. There was only a crack in the door. But, even if she did say something to him, what could she say? The woman has been kept isolated from Hossein Makfuf. She does not know the final plans. My name? Soviet armor? What could the American make of that? In any case, there is nothing she could say that would not incriminate herself. I am certain that we are simply faced with an immodest woman who could not control her instincts."

"I am not so confident, my dear Pirzadeh, but as you say, we have but two weeks left to wait. It would be difficult to stop us at this point."

"Only the American government . . ."

"I can hold them off for two weeks without difficulty," said the colonel with a sweep of his hand. "If they press the matter, I shall intervene with the gendarmerie and see that they launch a massive search of the area where the Americans were last seen. Shall we make it Bojnord?"

"An excellent idea. I will have their car driven to Bojnord and abandoned in the mountains."

"Just one more thing, Pirzadeh. We do not want the Americans to be killed."

"They will be safe, Colonel. My men will guard them well. We will be protected from them, and they will be protected from Ayatollah Shirazi."

Dr. Mohammad Hormozi waited impatiently for Jamshid Ansari to run the gauntlet of secretaries that protected the minister from unwelcome guests. As eagerly as he awaited the news he expected Ansari to bring him, he did not wish to have it appear that the young man's visit was in any way unusual.

At last Abbas Azad announced his arrival and showed him in. As soon as the door shut behind his visitor, Hormozi was pounding him with questions.

"Can it be done? What does your man say? What more does he need to know?"

For the first time since his initial visit to the minister's office, Jamshid felt he had the upper hand. He disdained the hard seat where supplicants were expected to sit and strolled to the end of the long carpet, where there was a seldom-used Louis Quinze sofa.

"Come here and sit with me, Dr. Hormozi. We have important matters to discuss."

Hormozi rarely allowed himself to be lured from behind his imposing desk, but his impatience drove him to set formalities aside.

"Can he do it?" he asked again as he took a seat beside Jamshid.

Jamshid nodded and smiled. "He can do it."

"How?"

"Before we get into that," Jamshid reached inside his suit coat and drew out a folded paper, "I have a document that you will have to sign to authorize the final arrangements." Hormozi looked wary. "You convinced me, Dr. Hormozi, when you told me how Ayatollah Pirzadeh and Colonel Ziya intended to betray us. We were naked. There was no way we could prevent them—except, of course, the way we have adopted. But, because you convinced me of the simplicity of one betrayal, we must take steps to prevent another. Therefore, I will ask you to put your signature to this order for the Shah's assassination—if you decide to order it."

171

Hormozi looked at the menacing paper and chewed on his lower lip. "First tell me the details."

"With pleasure. I'll leave the paper here between us. Now, the Shah's helicopter can be bombed without much difficulty. I have obtained the necessary materials from our friends in the Soviet Union. The bomb itself is inside a battery that looks like one of the helicopter's normal batteries. The batteries are checked before every flight, and our man can make the switch virtually at will. The battery with the bomb contains a real, more compact battery inside it also so that it tests out properly on the pre-flight check. The bomb's detonator is controlled in two steps by a miniaturized altimeter. As soon as the helicopter reaches a pre-set altitude, the bomb is armed; as soon as it drops below that altitude again, it explodes. It could explode going up too, of course; but you said you wanted it to blow up when it came into Nishapur, and this is the best way to arrange it." Jamshid fell silent.

"Is that all?" asked Hormozi after a few moments' silence. "What about the timing?"

"With this fuse, you don't need to time anything. Whenever the helicopter comes in for a landing, it will blow up. Of course, you set the altitude low enough to preclude an accident if it dips low en route. A hundred feet would probably be sufficient. The bomb itself is lethal; you won't be depending on the crash."

"It's really that simple," said Hormozi in wonderment.

"It's that simple. All you need is one perfectly placed fanatic, and that's just what we've got. We must let him know at least a week in advance so that he can ensure being on duty at the right time. Have you decided on a time?"

"I've been examining the report you received from your woman in Nishapur. The analysis is quite sound. I believe she's right. The climax of the passion play is the logical time for the Imam to be revealed. She says that the information she received indicates that the platform that Hossein Makfuf is supposed to deliver his final prayer from is armored. I suppose that means they'll have a bomb underneath the platform to make it look like he has miraculously survived. The only question is whether I can take the blind man's place at the proper moment."

"We'll do whatever we can to help you," said Jamshid. "As far as we can tell, Pirzadeh and his friends suspect nothing. They won't be taking too many precautions. Pirzadeh is even urging our central committee to be in Nishapur, no doubt so that we can be rounded up afterward when it comes time to slaughter the scapegoats."

"You must be careful that he doesn't carry out the slaughter before the roundup. But that would not be prudent." Hormozi picked up the assassination order that lay between them. "Ideally, the Shah's helicopter should explode just after the Twelfth Imam has been revealed. It will be another sign of God's favor. But it doesn't matter that much if it's off schedule. As long as it succeeds, it will prevent Pirzadeh and Ziya from putting their plans into action."

"There's no question about its success," said Jamshid confidently.

"If you mean that the bomb is certain to go off, you are probably right; but there is a long distance between that moment and final success. Still, an opportunity like this will never recur in our lifetimes." He pulled his silver felt-tipped pen from his inside coat pocket and signed the incriminating paper with a bold flourish. "It will never recur, Jamshid. It will never recur." He folded the paper and put it in his pocket with the pen.

"I believe the paper is for me," said Jamshid, holding out his hand.

"Not quite yet. You have seen me sign it. I will give it to you when I give you the final instructions for placing the bomb. But before that I must convince His Imperial Majesty to pay a visit to Nishapur."

CHAPTER **25**

The capture had gone smoothly. Ben Groves had found his way blocked by a disabled pickup truck as he bicycled down the deserted, windowless street that led from the Kamel residence toward the center of town. The men working on the vehicle had swiftly thrown a cloth sack over his head, bundled him into the truck's cab, and thrown his bicycle on behind. In less than a minute he had disappeared without a trace from the empty, dusty street. Scarcely an hour later Frank Quintana had descended the steps from the post office while sorting through the four envelopes he had just retrieved from his box. As soon as he had seated himself behind the wheel of his car, a muscular arm had encircled his neck from behind, and a callused hand had displayed a knife before his eyes. At the opening of the door on the driver's side, it had taken little coaxing by the arm around his neck to make him slide over and relinquish the driver's seat to a swarthy young man with a skullcap haircut. The car had pulled away from the post office at normal speed, and without attracting the slightest attention. Frank Quintana too had disappeared from Nishapur.

"I figured you'd show up sooner or later," said Groves dourly as Quintana was led into the small windowless room and his blindfold removed. The slam of the sturdy wooden door left them alone.

Frank looked frightened and quite pale. "Where are we? What's going to happen?"

Groves was reclining on a straw mat spread out along one wall. Half of the opposite wall was taken up with a rickety wooden table. Beneath it was an incongruously new-looking red plastic bucket. There was no other furniture in the room. Seeing that Frank had finished his initial terrified survey of their cell and was looking a bit more normal, Groves addressed himself to the questions he had asked.

"I can tell you where we are pretty well. They picked me up at about eleven o'clock, and I was here before noon. I could hear the noon call to prayer. It came from very close by."

"You mean we're near the mosque?" Nishapur's main mosque was in the center of the city.

"Nope. They use a recording there for the call to prayer. This was a real voice. I figure the only place it could be is the Mohammad Mahruq shrine. I'd even go so far as to guess that we're in some sort of storeroom out in the garden. The call was loud and clear as if there was nothing but that door between it and this room. If we were inside the shrine itself, it would be muffled."

The younger man looked blank. "Oh. I mean, that's very good reasoning. But what are we doing here? I suppose the door's locked."

"You can try it if you like," said Groves laconically. "My guess is that we have two guards. Either that, or we have one guard who keeps talking to himself. Unfortunately, that door's too thick to hear what they're saying. I doubt it would do us much good anyway, though."

Frank sank onto the mat and propped himself against the

dirty whitewashed wall. "You don't think they're going to . . ."

"Kill us? Not very likely. You're a diplomat; that would make it an international incident. My guess is that someone decided we were getting too snoopy and thought it would be best to put us away for the duration."

"Your heroic confrontation with that blind mulla must have gone too far," said Frank testily.

Groves looked offended but made no reply. The cobwebs on the ceiling engaged his eyes while his mind tried to figure out what sort of meal schedule their captors would maintain. He felt like asking the guards to send for something made personally by Mr. Kamel's wife. Eating her cooking without talking to her egregious husband would be a rare pleasure. He looked over to see how his fellow prisoner was adapting to the conditions of prison life. To his surprise, Frank was flipping the pages of a worn Agatha Christie paperback.

"Incredible. Ten minutes ago you were so scared your knees would barely hold you up. Now you're reading a detective story. Looks to me like a sign of shallowness of character." Groves was still smarting from the accusation that their incarceration was his fault. "Or am I wrong? What are you doing, just counting the pages?"

Frank gave him a condescending glance. "I'm deciphering a message from the embassy. I had just picked it up at the post office when they jumped me. This paperback is the key to a book code. I get a letter or telegram about my mother's illness, and I know it's got a coded message in it. Every word with a definite article in front of it is actually a number. You just substitute for each letter the number of its place in the alphabet, and you get one long number. The first three digits are the page number in the book; and remaining digits are the word number on the page."

"Sounds clumsy."

"It is. Particularly when you're making a message up. Some

numbers just can't be turned into words. If I have a lot to say, I just leave it in numbers and take a chance that my mail isn't being read." He flipped quickly to the back of the book and ran his finger slowly along the page.

"Is this the best the CIA can do?"

"No, it's just that I only had time for a short course."

Groves had slid closer and was looking over his shoulder. "I read *Murder in Mesopotamia* once. It's a good book. What number are you looking for?"

"Two thirty-six."

Groves silently watched Quintana's finger moving along each line. "Woman."

Frank looked up. "How do you know?"

"I counted."

"You have to do it with your finger or else you make mistakes." He went back to his counting. A minute later he wrote the word "woman" on the telegraph form in his lap.

"What's the next number?" asked Groves.

"That was the last one. Now I just have to put it together." He looked at the words scrawled on the form. "Bass—Tehran —maintenance—helicopter—Shah—full—security—clearance —no—connection—radical—woman."

"Are all of those words in *Murder in Mesopotamia*?"

"No. Names of characters in the book are code words for a list of specific names and terms that the CIA thought might be useful. 'Tehran' and 'Shah' for example. For a word like 'bass' you leave it uncoded the first time and then establish a code word for it."

"Where's the list of code words?"

"I memorized it. My God, are you nosy! I don't have to tell you any of this stuff!"

"I was just curious," said Groves. "May I ask one more question?"

"What?"

"What does the message mean?"

Frank held up the paper and studied it. "The problem is knowing where one thing stops and another begins. It seems to say that David Bass is working in Tehran on the maintenance of helicopters for the Shah. He has full security clearance and no connection with the radical woman."

"With what radical woman?"

"Zhaleh," murmured Frank under his breath.

"Who?"

"Zhaleh," he said louder.

"The pretty one you've been talking to? How do you know she's a radical? You told me you hadn't heard from the embassy about her." Groves was rapidly becoming indignant.

"I left some things out," replied Frank vaguely.

"Well, perhaps you should start putting them back in. I can make myself a very unpleasant cellmate if I think I'm being left in the dark about why I'm in here."

Frank's resistance was broken, and the remaining hours until dinner were occupied by a full narration of his relations with the beautiful radical, which blended imperceptibly into a heated argument over who was responsible for their imprisonment: Groves because of his confrontation with the would-be Hossein Makfuf, or Quintana because of his disclosure to Zhaleh of the details concerning the Moharram ceremonies and Groves's theory about the climax of the passion play.

It took a surprisingly appetizing dinner of steamed rice and a lamb-with-apricot stew to restore peace. In the lassitude induced by full stomachs they finally agreed upon four things: they didn't know why they had been taken prisoner; Frank had not been at fault for telling Zhaleh things that she could be expected to know already or at least have no difficulty finding out elsewhere; the message about her alleged boyfriend Bass told them nothing of importance; and there was no point in casting accusations at each other. With that, they turned to considering means of escape. But it was now quite dark, and the meal had been filling; before long they gave up and went to sleep along the one wall that conveyed warmth from a heated adjoining room.

Colonel Ziya was reading with deepening interest Ben Groves's field notes, which had been retrieved from the Kamel house by the police who had called there to investigate the disappearance of the two Americans. What he read was causing him alarm. The ring of the telephone on his desk startled him.

"Yes, I'll speak to the ambassador," he said in response to the message as to who was calling. There was a click as the connection was made. "Hello," he said in his heavily accented English.

"Am I speaking to the officer in charge of the search for Professor Benjamin Groves and Mr. Frank Quintana?"

"Yes. This is Colonel Ahmadi speaking." It was not the first time that Colonel Ziya had adopted the identity of a gendarme officer.

"This is Ralston Dermott, the American ambassador. I want a report on the progress of your investigation." The voice was exceedingly angry. "And please give me a specific reply. Otherwise I shall be forced to take this up with the Prime Minister."

"Certainly, Your Excellency. I can report that we have over five hundred gendarmes conducting the search. We have found the automobile that they were driving. It was in a mountainous area near Bojnord. We are searching that entire region, going to every village."

"What in the hell were they doing in Bojnord?"

"I don't know, Your Excellency. We have been examining the materials they left behind to see if there are any clues."

"What materials? Anything you have should have been sent to the American embassy."

"Yes, Your Excellency. We will send them right over, Mr. Ambassador."

"I want them here within the hour, do you understand? What is your name again?"

"Colonel Ahmadi, Mr. Ambassador. I will do whatever you say. At once, Your Excellency." There was a click as the connection was abruptly broken at the other end.

"However, I do not believe I will send over these interesting notes," said Colonel Ziya aloud to the empty office as he replaced the receiver.

CHAPTER **26**

A private audience with the Shah meant only that, for the few minutes allowed, the Minister of Culture and Art would have the Shah's complete attention. Despite himself, Hormozi shuddered as he was led by a protocol officer into the Shah's private office, its atmosphere heavy with gold draperies and ornately carved and gilded décor. He had shuddered on the occasion of his three previous private audiences, as well, but this time he tried to tell himself that there would be no more.

The imperial face, with its prominent nose and eyes deeply set beneath heavy brows, was as familiar a sight facing him across the vast expanse of polished mahogany desk as his own face was in his bathroom mirror, but the eyes seemed to bore into him nevertheless and chill his blood. As he stood waiting for the Shah to speak, he tried to recollect that it was the imperial pomp and grandeur that made such a profound impression and not the man himself. Any other person sitting in the same position would evoke the same feelings.

"We have read your report, Dr. Hormozi." The Shah's voice had a slightly epicene quality about it. "It is very persuasive. At first we were disappointed that you were intending to find the tombstone of Hossein Makfuf to be genuine. We thought we had made it clear that we were of the opposite opinion."

Hormozi kept his head slightly lowered. "Yes, Your Majesty. However, the records in the Ministry of Railroads confirmed the theory of the American professor. I had no choice."

"Records can be lost. That is something you might well remember in the future. But it is no matter now. As you point out in your report, what has happened is far better. We had not thought about the consequences of the decision you have finally reached, but it seems likely that you are right. Nishapur is destined to become a great city and center for pilgrimages. It will afford a magnificent opportunity for us to display our piety and our devotion to the faith. We have decided, therefore, to become the patron of the shrine of Hossein Makfuf as you proposed. We shall construct a mosque of such grandeur that in time Nishapur will equal Mashhad and Qom in holiness. You have made an excellent proposal, Dr. Hormozi. We congratulate you."

"Thank you, Your Majesty," said Hormozi.

"With regard to your suggestion that we come to Nishapur during the Moharram ceremonies and personally declare our belief in Hossein Makfuf and our thanks for the miracle of the discovery of his resting place, you were quite specific in your timetable. We prefer the fifth and sixth of Moharram to the fourth and fifth."

"Your Majesty, the schedule of the ceremonies cannot be changed at this late date. There are tens of thousands of pilgrims whose movements and needs must be accommodated. To change the schedule now would cause turmoil in the plans and possibly lead to an unruly crowd."

"Then the fourth and fifth it shall be. You suggest that we arrive at four o'clock. What will the schedule be like after that?"

"The drama of the martyrdom of Hossein Makfuf will end at

four o'clock, Your Majesty. The pilgrims will all be at the prayer grounds. This will allow Your Majesty to come in by helicopter to the guesthouse at the Omar Khayyam monument without interference from a throng of people. By Your Majesty's gracious favor, I myself will be staying at the guesthouse and will ensure that all is prepared there for a reception and banquet that will begin at eight o'clock. All of the dignitaries in Khurasan will be attending the drama and will come to the reception after the crowd disperses. On the morning of the fifth, at ten o'clock, Your Majesty will deliver a speech declaring Your Majesty's patronage of the Hossein Makfuf shrine. Departure will follow at Your Majesty's convenience."

"Security will be difficult," the Shah said.

"The people will be pilgrims, Your Majesty, and Your Majesty's visit will be a complete surprise. The Omar Khayyam guesthouse is situated quite near the prayer grounds. I am certain that the usual precautions will be adequate."

"We were thinking of the stupid propaganda for the Twelfth Imam, Dr. Hormozi."

"Mere foolishness, Your Majesty. The work of religious fanatics. When God chooses to send the Twelfth Imam, He will not notify us in advance with posters pasted on walls during the night."

The Shah's wide mouth pulled still wider in an ironic smile. "Let us hope that He gives us *some* warning, Dr. Hormozi. We must have time to prepare ourselves for the end of the world. For our visit to Nishapur, our Minister of Court will arrange further matters with your ministry. We congratulate you again on your ingenious thought."

"Thank you, Your Majesty," replied Hormozi as he began backing with lowered head toward the door of the office.

Once outside Hormozi walked rapidly down the long path through the garden that was used by private visitors to the palace. He was smiling inwardly at the Shah's imperial performance. The report he had submitted had been full of figures on the availability of cheap land in what was destined to become

183

the great pilgrimage city of Nishapur, and he had no doubt that the Shah's agents were already at work buying it up for the benefit of the imperial pocketbook. But the Shah had not given the slightest hint that he had even noticed such mundane matters. If fate destined a successful outcome for his plans, it would not be long before he, too, Mohammad Hormozi, would be able to practice such mercenary behavior on an imperial scale.

In Washington, Bill Keller's background paper for a presidential decision memorandum had been redrafted several times. Each time Emmanuel Holachek had grunted and handed it back. This time he seemed happier.

"It's come a long way since you first took a look at it, hasn't it, Bill?"

"Iran isn't exactly my specialty," replied his assistant.

"I know, but look here: first time around you concluded that the Shah was indispensable to the integrity of the free world; this time you seem to think he's a threat to all we hold dear."

"I was able to look at it in a larger perspective this time. You'll notice the part about a probable economic and military alliance between Saudi Arabia and a conservative religious government in Iran. I think that's something that should be emphasized. If the conservative Muslims got together and decided that the U.S. was the best safeguard against Communism, it would probably guarantee leverage over oil prices for the foreseeable future. In addition, we can sell arms to the Iranians to protect the oil fields without pissing off the Israelis the way we do when we sell them to the Saudis."

"How about the Israelis? Would a religious government in Iran upset them?"

"Probably. Almost everything does. But the Iranians have a good record with the Israelis. It might add up to useful pressure from our point of view. Another thing to notice, of course, is the tie-in with Pakistan. The Paks have a strong religious streak in them, and the tighter they get with Iran, the more the Soviets are isolated in Afghanistan."

184

"In other words, your hypothetical Twelfth Imam government could lend stability to the entire area."

"That, and it would also finesse any succession problem in the near future—assuming, that is, that Hormozi is our man."

"How's that shaping up over at CIA?"

"Kaufman seems at a loss. He says there's almost nothing going on that would indicate that a coup is about to be sprung. He's afraid that the SAVAK people in Tehran are deliberately keeping CIA in the dark. The only positive indicator is from a little blonde working for the Iran-America Society. She reports that Dr. Hormozi is so nervous he can't make it in bed any more. I don't suppose that's something the President needs to know. Still, it's intelligence of a sort."

"And your old friend we sent out as an amateur spy?"

"I apologize for that one. Your first opinion of it was right. It looks like a fiasco. Frank Quintana's too much of a bureaucrat for cloak-and-dagger work, I guess. But Ambassador Dermott is delighted—or rather, was delighted. Quintana spent a few days in Tehran after he arrived and then went out to Nishapur to talk to an old professor of his who was working there."

"What did he do that for?"

"Don't know. He seemed to think it would tell him something about Freddy Desuze. Our little blonde seems to think Frank isn't too bright. In any case, he stayed in Nishapur—to Dermott's delight—for over two weeks. What for we don't know."

"Then what?"

"He and the professor both disappeared. Dermott has been cracking heads in the gendarmerie to find out where they disappeared to, but no luck so far."

Holachek looked pensive. "Looks like I'm going to take some heat on this one. I shouldn't have let you talk me into it. Did the guy ever send in any reports?"

"Two. He asked about an Iranian woman who has a record in this country as a student radical and is on the CIA list as an underground member of the Muslim Marxist Alliance in Tehran. They don't know her current whereabouts. The other was a query about an American who might have been her boyfriend. He's working now in Tehran servicing the Shah's helicopters." Holachek cocked an eyebrow. "He's okay apparently. Excellent war record in Vietnam. Top security clearance. Clean-living, upright specimen of American manhood; and no record of a connection with the Iranian woman."

"Could it have been missed?"

"Kaufman's checking on that. Of course, we don't know what made Frank Quintana ask about these people. If he reappears, maybe we'll find out."

"*When* he reappears. Government officials are always optimistic. You can file that background report, by the way. I think we have enough to go on if we need it."

Moharram:
The Sixth Month

Dawn on the first day of Moharram brought with it a cool, clear blue sky marred only by a scattering of cloud fluffs over the mountains. The field of tents, which had expanded beyond its intended borders, was teeming with people. The influx in the previous two days had exceeded expectations, and the lines of pilgrims waiting their turn at the water outlets were cruelly long. Yet there was an aura of quiet tenseness, of hopeful waiting, that seemed to dampen the potentially explosive irritations that the crowding inevitably brought with it. Gendarmes had been brought in to assist the small force of local police in keeping order, but they studiously remained on the fringes of the pilgrim mass.

The order of events called for communal noon prayers for men only at Nishapur's primary mosque and at the shrine mosque of Mohammad Mahruq. Women would be accommodated in smaller groups at a number of minor neighborhood mosques. Following the prayers would come sermons by a series of mullas telling the story of Hossein, the martyred Third

Imam, and for the first time in history adding the story of his supposedly martyred great-grandson Hossein Makfuf. Evening would see the first of the daily processions of mourning through the city's illuminated streets. Succeeding days would follow a similar pattern, with the focus shifting on the third day to the newly prepared prayer grounds at the shrine of Hossein Makfuf. There a day of sermons and storytelling would be followed by a day-long reenactment of the tragic history of the failed rebellion of the saint's father Zaid and the subsequent murder of father, brother Yahya, and finally the blind saint himself. On the fifth day would come the ceremonial hallowing of the shrine with a sermon from the Minister of Culture and Art, and the remainder of the ten-day period of religious devotion would be occupied with a shortened version of the customary drama and mourning ceremonies for the Third Imam.

All of this was well known to the two prisoners in the storeroom cell at the shrine of Mohammad Mahruq. Groves had spent much of the preceding week and a half fuming over being prevented from observing the events that should comprise the climax of his study. Frank Quintana had even begun to wonder whether the professor was identifying too closely with Hossein Makfuf. The image of Dr. Frankenstein being destroyed by the monster he had created came to mind, but it did not seem like a fit topic for conversation.

For his own part, Frank had spent his time diligently searching for a way of escaping from the storeroom. He had measured it time and again and had pounded on every accessible inch of the walls and floor, hoping for a mysterious hollow sound. He had discovered that the flimsy table, when disassembled, provided nothing of sufficient weight and solidity to be a plausible weapon, and they had been left with a small heap of wood in one corner of the room. The plastic bucket and the mat held no greater promise. The only glimmer of hope came from the thrice-daily visits of servant women who brought their food and emptied the plastic bucket. Unfortunately, there were invariably two guards at the door during such moments.

Groves had provided little cooperation after a brief initial survey had convinced him that there was no way for them to leave the storeroom until they were released. He had infuriated his fellow prisoner by not mentioning that he carried a pocket knife until a week after their imprisonment, when he produced it to pare his fingernails. Reluctantly, Frank had had to admit that he did not feel up to attacking two athletic young men with a single three-inch blade.

On the first day of Moharram the noises of worshipers streaming into the garden around the shrine could be heard long before the noon call to prayer. Frank had once been enthusiastic about the possibility of escaping and melting into the crowd, but now the noises were simply frustratingly tantalizing as he reclined dejectedly on the mat. Just as the call to prayer began with a nasal, melodic assertion of God's greatness, the key sounded in the padlock outside their door. The usual blinding shaft of light that augured the arrival of lunch cut across the room, and the dark outline of a chadur-clad woman carrying a tray appeared in the doorway.

As she put the tray down, she said softly but clearly in English, "I'll get you out of here tomorrow morning."

Frank jerked himself erect and peered into the shadowed face concealed by the margins of the chadur. Zhaleh's beautiful large eyes peered back at him. A finger at her lips stifled any response. In a moment she was gone. The voice of the muezzin could still be heard melodiously summoning the pious to their devotions.

"Your girlfriend?" asked Groves.

Frank nodded. "I guess you were right about her acting as a servant here."

"How is she going to let us out?"

"You heard everything I heard."

As the prayers in the shrine ended and the first of the series of mullas mounted the narrow wooden pulpit to begin the first round of sermons, three figures separated themselves from the

191

rest of the throng and ascended a stone stairway to a second-floor arcade. At the end of the walkway the shrine's senior mulla bowed his honored guests into his spartan office. The aged Ayatollah Shirazi seemed even older than usual and badly winded by the flight of stairs. He sat for several minutes on a metal folding chair breathing deeply while the other two respectfully waited for him to recover. When he had breath enough to speak he turned to Pirzadeh.

"If you have captured them, Pirzadeh, you *must* kill them. I insist upon it. When it is all over, they will be a danger to us because of what they know and what they will learn."

The younger mulla surveyed the white-bearded elder through his black-rimmed glasses. "They know nothing of importance. I have given my men orders that they are not to be harmed. Colonel Ziya has arranged to have them arrested for spying immediately after the ceremonies and expelled from the country."

The old man shook his head. "So your men keep the Americans in the prison and everyone else out of it. It seems you are in control, Pirzadeh. Well, then, you must be certain that they are not found outside their prison; I do not think it would be safe for them."

Pirzadeh ignored the threat and turned toward the third mulla, who was pulling nervously at his scraggly salt-and-pepper beard. "Is all in readiness? The explosives, have they been placed as you were instructed?"

"Your own men supervised the placement, Ayatollah Pirzadeh. I have done everything precisely as you directed."

"Then, if God wills, nothing will go wrong. The custodian of the shrine, will he do his job? We depend upon him entirely."

"He is completely reliable, your worship. He suspects nothing and knows nothing."

"They had better not be caught outside their prison," interrupted the white-bearded old man, who followed his statement with a scratchy laugh that ended in a fit of coughing.

A hundred meters from the Mohammad Mahruq shrine

across the adjoining garden of the Omar Khayyam monument, Dr. Mohammad Hormozi was just arriving in a ministry car that had picked him up at the airport in Mashhad. The car had stopped once at a prearranged spot on the outskirts of Nishapur to pick up an additional passenger, Jamshid Ansari. The two men had carried on an ordinary cordial discussion during the remaining brief trip to the Shah's Omar Khayyam guesthouse, since the ministry car did not have a window between the passenger's and the driver's seat. Not until they had locked themselves inside the end apartment of the guesthouse did they mention the topic that was uppermost in their minds.

"Is everything prepared, Jamshid?" asked the minister with evident nervousness.

"We have done everything that can be done. Zhaleh has seen the blind mulla. He is staying at Mohammad Mahruq. He will come to the platform from a rear stairway at the end of a path between the two shrines. You will be seated on the opposite side on a platform reserved for notables. You will have to make your way to the stairway before the end of the play. As long as they suspect nothing, the substitution should be simple. When a mulla appears on top of the platform, whoever he may be, we expect the bomb to be exploded."

Hormozi placed his hands on the carved back of a chair to steady their shaking. His mouth was dry. "You are sure the explosion will be safe?"

Jamshid contained a desire to sneer at the minister's cowardice. "To you it will be entirely safe. The platform is completely armored. I dressed as a pilgrim and managed to inspect it myself yesterday. The blast will be deflected downward and out the front and sides. Anyone behind or on top will be unharmed."

"And those in front and on the sides?"

"There will be casualties," said Jamshid. "There must be casualties to make your survival a convincing miracle. The bomb will probably have a minimum of shrapnel, however. With luck, the deaths will not be many."

"How many?" Jamshid shrugged his shoulders. "What about afterward? Have you done as I asked?"

Jamshid nodded. "Everyone in the Mohammad Mahruq shrine will be killed immediately after the blast when the confusion is greatest. Zhaleh has given us a plan of the building, and she will command the operation. The surprise should be total. Mullas, servants, the entire nest will be cleared out. After your revelation, I will speak to the crowd about the goals of the revolution while you come back here. The radio transmitter in the Shah's suite is powerful enough to be heard throughout the country. You will be able to announce the Shah's death and the Twelfth Imam's reappearance. Our friends will begin street demonstrations in the name of the Twelfth Imam in every city the moment they hear your announcement. Will you know how to operate the radio?"

For the first time in days Hormozi gave one of his flashing smiles. "I didn't waste my time entirely when I was at Caltech. One of the things I have learned is that whoever controls the radio controls people's minds, but the person who controls the radio is not simply the person who speaks over it but also the person who knows how to make it operate."

"Then we are prepared," murmured Jamshid confidently.

Jamshid turned to the door. "I must leave. I will not see you again until the day." He waited to see if Hormozi was going to reply. Then Jamshid slipped quickly out the door and ran the few steps that separated him from the car. Acting on prior instructions, the driver departed as soon as his passenger had entered.

Alone in the small but ornately furnished bedroom, Mohammad Hormozi was sitting on the end of the silk-covered bed staring fixedly at nothing at all. His fingers were carefully fingering a string of ivory prayer beads. He was very pale. A single sentence he had once said to Ansari passed over and over again through his mind: "The opportunity will never recur in our lifetimes . . . the opportunity will never recur in our lifetimes . . ."

CHAPTER 28

Throughout Iran religious fervor began to build as the traditional Moharram mourning ceremonies entered their second day. Companies of men from the different craft and trade guilds paraded in the streets with bared chests, which they beat rhythmically with their hands and with thin chains as they chanted prayers and called out the names of the martyred Imams. In every town, large and small, the mosques were filled with tearful worshipers listening with rapt attention to the traditional recital of the martyrs' agonies of thirteen centuries before. Daily the emotion and the drama would intensify until the climactic tenth day, when the entire country would reach a religious catharsis of prayer and weeping.

Only in Nishapur was the time-honored pattern varied to accommodate the cult of the miraculously revealed martyr Hossein Makfuf. As Ben Groves paced the small storeroom in tense anticipation, he wondered whether he could still complete his investigation of just what it was that drove certain people to flock to a new pilgrimage site and embrace a new cult figure.

Frank Quintana's thoughts were on the more immediate future. What would they do if Zhaleh succeeded in releasing them? What would happen to her?

At precisely ten-fifteen there was a dull, heavy noise at the bottom of the door. Seconds passed. They heard the padlock being unlocked, and the door swung slowly inward.

"Drag him inside," came the sharp command from the woman in the doorway. With the sun behind her, the woman's face was lost in shadow, but the voice was Zhaleh's. Both prisoners leaped forward and grabbed at the slumped body of the guard, who had already fallen part way inside the room with the opening of the door. Frank suddenly dropped the arm he was pulling at when he saw blood drooling with a bubbling noise from the man's mouth.

"Have you killed him?" He now noticed that Zhaleh was holding a long butcher knife in her right hand.

"I assume so," she replied automatically. "Get him inside before the other one comes back from the toilet. I've been waiting all morning for him to go."

Groves had already succeeded in manhandling the body into the room and was trying to pull him around the door so that he could not be seen from the outside. Frank felt nauseated. The blood was leaving a trail on the dusty floor, and the bubbling noise was still coming from his throat.

"They'll never learn that a woman can be dangerous," said Zhaleh contemptuously. "Stay in here. The other one must be on his way back."

With that she stepped outside and took up a position facing the open door, her left hand raised to her mouth as if in horror. She seemed to totter on the verge of fainting. They heard the sounds of heavy footsteps running on gravel, and then she was looking to her left and pointing into the room. A second later and a man's silhouette appeared in the door frame, crouched and ready for whatever was inside. There was a loud thump, and he fell forward into the room, the hilt of the butcher knife protruding from the left side of his back. Frank Quintana vomited onto the mat.

Groves again pulled the body the rest of the way into the storeroom and then looked to Zhaleh for instructions. He seemed perfectly calm.

From a basket on the ground outside she produced two folded pieces of black cloth. "Put these over your heads. I'll hide you in the pantry in the shrine, and you can try slipping out with the pilgrims who leave after the noon prayer." Groves looked at the wide expanse of garden they would have to walk across to get to the side door of the shrine. "Walk with small steps and hunch over a little bit. From a distance you should be mistaken for servants."

Groves's chadur lacked six inches of reaching the ground, but Frank was completely swathed when they stepped from the storeroom. Zhaleh fastened the padlock behind them and slid the key under the door. With small, shuffling steps the two men followed her across the garden, not daring to look to see whether anyone was within sight. The side door of the shrine was the same one the little custodian of Hossein Makfuf had used to admit Groves to the mullas' lounge three months earlier. The kitchen was the first room they had to pass. None of the three women engaged in cooking the mullas' lunch looked up from her work. At the next door Zhaleh stopped and produced an old-fashioned hand-crafted key. The lock turned with a shrill squeak. The heavy door opened inward, and a cloud of musty vegetable smells issued from the dark interior. The three hurried inside, and Zhaleh pushed the door shut behind them.

Her voice was stern and commanding. "You must stay in here until I let you out. I'm going to lock you in and keep the key. No one else will be able to enter. When I let you out, you will leave by the door you came in by and mingle with the pilgrims. Leave the chadurs here; women would be even more conspicuous than Americans. If they've discovered you're missing by then and are guarding the gate, stick to the center of the crowd, and you'll still have a chance."

"What about you?" asked Frank, touching her arm in the semidarkness.

"I have work to do here," she replied coldly. "This is a revolution. Haven't you grasped that by now? I'm a revolutionary. In two days the Shah will be dead and Iran will enter a new era. My job is to see to it that every mulla and servant in this shrine is killed. If you are here then, you will be killed too. I can't waste my time protecting you."

Frank could only stare at the dim face he felt he had known.

"Why are you letting us go?" asked Groves laconically. "Suppose we go to the police. Or are you the little cold-blooded terrorist with a heart of gold?"

"Frank helped me without asking questions when I needed help. I feel you deserve a chance." Her voice was calm and steady. "Actually, I don't think you'll make it. The shrine is too well guarded. But at least you'll have a chance. I've done what I can. As for warning anyone, our people control every means of communication in Nishapur. There's no way you can send a message to anyone. I'm going now." In a softer voice she added, "Good luck, Frank." He didn't reply.

"Nice girlfriend you've got," Groves remarked as soon as the squeak of the lock had been heard.

"She's a murderer," said Frank in astonishment. "What she did to those men, it made me sick."

"So I noticed. That doesn't help us now, though, does it? The question is how to get out of this alive."

"No, the question is how to give a warning to the embassy." Frank's tone had suddenly become almost normal.

"You think she was lying about the communications?"

"Not at all. But you once told me that Freddy Desuze's radio is somewhere in this building. It has a special circuit built into it for communicating directly with the embassy. Did I ever tell you Desuze was a CIA agent? If we can find the radio, we can still give a warning."

"And get killed in the process. Though finding the radio's no problem. If it's still there, it's in a little tearoom right down this hallway. The problem is that whatever chance we've got will be lost if we stay to fiddle around with it."

"Can we grab it and run?"

"It would be hard. It's a big thing, and there's an antenna wire running out of it. Without the antenna, you probably couldn't call Sabzavar, much less Tehran."

"Then we'll have to take the chance."

"You can take it alone. You're the diplomat. It's none of my business."

"Think how grateful the Shah would be to the man who saved his life."

There was a long pause.

"What do we do with your girlfriend?"

"Lock her in here and take the key. Maybe we can find something to tie her up with."

There was no more to say. A half hour's search through dimly seen jars and baskets yielded nothing that could be used for bonds. They were still looking when the lock squeaked again. The task of subduing her had been assumed by Groves. It took one blow from behind with a heavy pottery jug to accomplish the task. By sudden inspiration they tore her cotton chadur into strips and used them to tie her wrists and ankles.

The deserted hallway indicated that the prayers had yet to be finished. The tearoom was equally empty. But in the corner behind the door stood the incongruously modern radio. As Groves shut the door to the hallway he heard a distant pounding. He stuck his head into the hallway long enough to discover that the sound came not from the pantry where they had left Zhaleh but from the storeroom on the far side of the garden, where a handful of men were watching axes being applied to the stout door.

"They're about to discover we've escaped," he whispered.

Crouched in the corner, Frank was turning dials with shaking fingers. "This shouldn't take long. It's like a combination. You set three dials on the right numbers, and the broadcast circuit is opened."

"That doesn't look like a transmitter to me," whispered Groves.

"It's not supposed to look like a transmitter. This smaller speaker is actually a microphone. They told me you just have to speak into it." Static was now issuing from the radio. "Calling the American embassy in Tehran," said Frank tentatively.

"It looks like you're talking to your radio," observed Groves.

"Calling the American embassy in Tehran."

"This is the American embassy in Tehran," came a crackling response. "Who is speaking?"

"This is Frank Quintana, Assistant Vice-Consul Frank Quintana. Do you understand me?"

"We read you, Frank Quintana. This is a scrambler circuit. Do you have an emergency?"

Both men were in thrall to the crackling voice. "Yes, emergency. In two days the Shah will be assassinated. Possibly by David Bass, a helicopter mechanic. There is going to be a coup."

"Say again, Frank Quintana."

Suddenly the door to the room burst open and then shut. Both men's hearts leaped in their place of concealment behind the door.

"That was too quick; they'll look again," said Groves.

"Say again, Frank Quintana," came the voice on the radio. "Where are you calling from?"

"We've got to go," whispered Groves urgently. "The hallway is the only way out." Quintana spun the three dials and flipped the power switch.

There were no sounds at the door. Cautiously they pulled it open and looked out. Three men were standing at the end of the hallway facing toward the garden. As quietly as possible Groves and Quintana stepped into the hallway and turned in the opposite direction. A right-angle turn took them out of sight. Momentarily relieved, they walked warily toward the darkness at the corridor's end. As they drew closer, they realized that beyond lay the shrine's great domed sanctuary. The sound of communal prayers filtered dimly into the corridor.

"They'll spot us as soon as we go in there," whispered Frank.

At that moment the turbaned head of a mulla appeared at the entrance to the sanctuary and as quickly disappeared again.

"I think we've been spotted already," whispered Groves. "Let's try for the kitchen. There may be a window."

Before they had reached the turning that had brought them into the corridor, they heard the running footsteps of several men behind them. A look over the shoulder revealed two turbaned servants with drawn pistols followed by a scurrying brown-robed mulla. Suddenly they were at the corner and around it, but the three men who had been at the door to the garden were no longer there. Instead they were twelve feet away just coming out of the tearoom. Quintana and Groves stopped dead in their tracks. There was no place to run. The three men, who looked like the storeroom guards, completely filled the hallway as they advanced slowly toward them.

Suddenly the noise behind them increased as their other pursuers rounded the corner. They turned around and saw the guns being raised. Then there was a torrent of motion as the men blocking the hallway charged past the Americans on either side and violently tackled the men with the guns. Arriving late on the scene, the slippered mulla beat a hasty retreat as soon as he saw the flailing tangle of bodies on the floor. But the fight was over almost as soon as it had started. Both of the armed men were inert on the stone pavement, their weapons in the hands of their three assailants. Neither Groves nor Quintana had made a move during the brief struggle. They remained rooted to the spot as the triumphant trio ominously approached. One of the Iranians ordered them in Persian to turn around. Having no other choice, they turned their backs. Frank heard the crack of a pistol butt hitting Groves's head a second before a similar blow turned his own world dark.

CHAPTER **29**

The communications clerk had been summoned peremptorily to the ambassador's office.

"Are you certain this is the exact message received?" boomed the ambassador's stentorian voice.

"Yes, Sir, as close as I can make out. I replayed the tape several times to check my copy. But the signal was not entirely clear. He must have been broadcasting without much of an antenna."

"You wouldn't have made a mistake on words like 'assassinated' or 'Shah,' would you?"

"No, Sir."

"Because if you have . . ." The threat was left hanging as the ambassador turned to his desk. "This is a cable I want sent immediately to Washington, highest priority." He handed a piece of paper to the clerk.

"Yes, Sir."

As the clerk left, Susan Bengston was waiting to enter. The

ambassador's secretary pulled the door closed behind her.

"Miss Bengston, I'm sorry to call you over here so urgently." Cordiality had replaced the bombast of moments before. "The consul's office tells me that an American civilian has been taking Persian lessons at the Iran-America Society. I want to find out everything I can about him."

"There are a lot of Americans in our Persian courses, Sir. I certainly don't know them all. I could find out who his teacher is, though." It passed through her mind that the ambassador's inquiry was not the sort to justify a pell-mell dash to the embassy through north Tehran traffic. "Perhaps you don't want our Iranian faculty involved, however."

"That's a very astute observation, Miss Bengston. Very astute. The man's name is David Bass." Her face registered nothing. "I need to find out everything about him in the next twenty-four hours. In particular, whom he associates with, how he spends his time, what he talks about—political information is what I'm looking for."

"Aren't there other . . ."

"Our usual security people must not be seen to do anything unusual. This embassy must appear completely normal. We're dealing with a possible assassination, Miss Bengston. We have, at most, two days. It could well be a false alarm, but if it isn't, we don't want the timetable to be advanced because of foolish moves on our part. You appreciate our situation."

"Yes, Sir. I should be able to report to you tomorrow morning." She looked at her watch. There was still time to find out who David Bass's Persian teacher was before the late-afternoon classes began.

"Two of my men are dead!" cried Pirzadeh vehemently at his white-bearded superior sitting crosslegged on the floor. "If you tell me that you did not order your servants to kill them and then kill the Americans, I tell you that you are lying!" His long brown robe swirled as he turned on the old man. "You are lying!"

Piercing brown eyes set in nests of wrinkles looked up at him from under the old man's turban. "If *I* had ordered it, the Americans would be dead too," came the croaked reply.

"Your servants bungled it! They bungled it, and then tried to hide the bodies. It was only the turn of fate that put the Americans back in my hands before your assassins found them."

"You have always been too rash, Pirzadeh. My servants had nothing to do with the killings. It is true that they would have killed the Americans if they had found them, but they would never trade two Muslim souls for two Christian ones."

"Then who did kill my men?"

The old man stared straight ahead. "The Communist woman."

"That's impossible. The Americans tied her and locked her in the kitchen pantry. They had the key with them when we captured them. Her head is lacerated from being struck down from behind. Can you truly believe that she set them free, and in return they did that to her?"

"It's the only possibility," rasped the old mulla.

"I refuse to believe it."

"She fornicated with the American. She is an evil woman, a Communist. She should be killed whether she helped them escape or not."

"That may be, but it can wait a few days longer. She will be arrested with the other Communists and executed."

Suddenly there were tears in the aged eyes. "We must not quarrel amongst ourselves," said the old man in a tremulous voice. "Our great stroke to return Iran to the ways of true religion must not fall short because of our quarreling."

Pirzadeh was touched by the fragile sentimentality of the plea. "We shall not quarrel. We shall not quarrel," he replied softly. "We shall destroy the Communists and bring the godless Shah under our control. Nothing can prevent our success."

"Then kill the Americans," came the sobbing, grating response.

Pirzadeh's face hardened. "No. They are in my custody. You cannot find them. I will not allow them to be killed."

"Where are we?" Frank felt cold soil under his hands. It was very dark.

"What month is it?"

Frank was conscious of a throbbing pain over his right ear. "It's Moharram. Where are we?" His body was cold.

"What's my name?"

"Ben Groves. What the hell is going on?" He tried to rise on one elbow, and the pain above his ear sharpened. He eased himself back. "Won't you tell me where the hell we are?" he said plaintively.

"I was just trying to find out if you were lucid," said Groves with an unaccustomed touch of sympathy in his voice. "You've been asking where we are for hours, and every time I tell you, you forget and ask all over again. It's gotten boring. I think you suffered a concussion when you got hit. Last time I asked you what my name was you said Billy Wilson."

"I did? He was a roommate I had in college. Look, am I lucid enough now for you to tell me where we are? I don't want to bore you." The throbbing was growing intense again.

"We're underground someplace in the ruins."

"Underground? You mean buried?" Frank's voice was tinged with fear.

"No. It's dark because it's night. The ruins are full of pits dug by treasure hunters. They're like wells. When the diggers hit the level of the medieval city, usually at around fifteen to twenty feet, they dig little galleries into the sides of the pit to look for whatever is left in the building they happen to have dug into. It's like mining. Pottery, coins, jewelry—they find all sorts of stuff they can sell to the Tehran antique dealers. We've been put into one of their holes. We're in one of the galleries dug into the side at the bottom. It's the only place there's room to lie down. Unfortunately, you can't stand up. Don't try, or you'll hit your head."

"I'm not about to try," said Frank weakly.

"There are guards at the top of the pit. Otherwise, I think it's narrow enough for us to climb out."

"I'm thirsty."

Groves placed the loop handle of a water jug in his hand. "We have food, too, if you feel hungry. They lowered down a full meal. The rice is cold, though."

"I'm not hungry." Frank let out a low moan. "My head feels terrible. Why didn't they kill us? We were trapped, weren't we?"

"I haven't the slightest idea. The boys who had us boxed in attacked each other instead of us. That's the last thing I remember."

"Where are we?"

Frank heard a sigh in the dark. "What month is it?" came Groves's tired voice.

"No, I don't mean where are we in the ground. I mean where are we in the ruins?"

"Oh, I thought you had drifted off again. We must be not too far from Mohammad Mahruq. The call to prayer sounded fairly loud. This pit kills any sense of direction, though."

For a long time there was nothing said. Frank's breathing took on the rhythm of sleep.

Susan Bengston had had no difficulty introducing herself to a group of Americans bent on learning Persian and struggling to make up practice conversations in the society's hamburger bar. They were only too eager to vent their complaints to the person in charge of the language program. The problem had been to channel the conversation in the direction she wanted. But her problem had been eased by the information the Iranian teacher had given her that David Bass was the best student in the class, though he had stopped coming a week before without explana-

206

tion. After attempting a couple of questions about the source of Bass's success and getting only bland responses, she happened to ask whether he possibly did better than the others because he had a secret Iranian girlfriend. That hit the jackpot.

"It's not a secret any more," volunteered a red-haired member of the class who had introduced himself as Steve. "Last time he was here—it must have been over a week ago—he bent my ear for an hour after class talking about an old Iranian girlfriend of his that he was going back to. I don't know how long ago they broke up, but I guess he needs her back now that we're coming to the subjunctives."

"Don't try it, Steve," remarked one of the women. "You're a married man."

"You don't know the girl's name, do you?" asked Susan with all the innocence she could muster.

"Zhaleh. He kept chanting it into his beer, 'Zhaleh, Zhaleh, Zhaleh.' Zhaleh Hekmat. Why, did you think it was one of the teachers?"

"You never can tell," said Susan with a laugh. "As you know, our teaching staff is renowned for its beauty."

The comment evoked general laughter from the men and polite smiles from the women.

CHAPTER 30

The beginning of the third day of Moharram found Susan Bengston in the outer office of Dr. Mohammad Hormozi. His secretary, Abbas Azad, was perplexed by her unexpected visit.

"You see, Abbas, Dr. Hormozi wanted me to find out some information about a certain girl. He is sure there is a file on her here."

"But why he did not telephone me if he wanted?" replied the secretary in Iran-America Society English.

"He had personal reasons," said Susan ambiguously.

"I would have come and found last night." Abbas's face was a portrait of dejection. "Why from Nishapur he wants to know this?"

"I don't think that's a question he would want me to answer," returned Susan with an edge to her voice. Then she allowed a conspiratorial smile to come over her face and added in a suggestive way, "He has found a girl there he is interested in."

Abbas looked shocked. His face reddened. "He called *you*, Miss Bengston?"

Susan struggled to cover a smirk with a woman-of-the-world look. "The minister and I understand such things," she said aloofly.

The young secretary avoided her eyes and reached for the slip of paper she had been holding in her hand. "I will look," he said coldly.

Twenty minutes passed. Susan's hope that such a file might exist somewhere in the bowels of the ministry began to dim. The enlarged engravings of Iranian mosques decorating the office no longer held her attention, but she continued to stare at one and then another as she considered the consequences of her gamble. On the debit side, her relationship with Mohammad Hormozi would surely be at an end. His performance had been distinctly flaccid in recent weeks, however, and the time might well be ripe for a change. On the credit side, the praise of Ambassador Dermott might do even more for her career than sleeping with an Iranian cabinet minister had done.

After thirty-five minutes the secretary returned. He had a manila file folder in his hand.

"What information does Dr. Hormozi want?" he asked after seating himself at his desk. He opened the file. "The woman was student in the United States on ministry scholarship."

"What the minister wants to know is a private matter between him and me, Abbas." Susan Bengston was holding her hand out imperiously for the file. "I will read it in his office, in private."

The secretary glared at her as he handed over the file. Stiffly he walked to the door of the inner office and held it open for her to go in. His mind was teeming with thoughts of the utter depravity of blonde women, light blonde foreign women who were no better than prostitutes.

"How are you feeling?" asked Groves as Frank began to stir beneath the blankets belatedly supplied by the guards. "You slept a long time. I have some breakfast for you if you feel up to it."

Frank tentatively reached out and touched the makeshift bandage that had been applied to his head. The dim morning light that penetrated to their subterranean lair was sufficient for Groves to see him wince at the touch.

"I felt pretty good until I touched it." He began to sit up.

"Watch your head; this is a low ceiling."

Frank carefully maneuvered himself to a semi-sitting posture slouched against a crumbly dirt wall. "At least it's dry down here. What's for breakfast?"

"I have a dish of yogurt, two hard-boiled eggs, and an orange. No tea."

"I'll try the yogurt." He accepted the pottery bowl extended to him and skimmed off the skin that had formed on its contents.

"I figured something out," said Groves as he watched him eat.

"What's that?"

"I think this level we're at must be ninth century. Look at these broken pieces of pottery. This plain white with aubergine glaze calligraphy must be ninth century. Maybe tenth."

"I'm happy you've been making good use of your time," said Frank sarcastically. "Have you had time to think of a way for us to get out of here?"

"There isn't any way—unless you feel like tunneling. They're sitting right at the top of the well. You can see their shadows on the side up there. One of them even told me that they're protecting us from some other folks who want to kill us. I think it was meant as an added inducement for us to stay in our hole."

"You mean we just sit down here until they decide to let us out?"

"That's about the size of it."

"I think I'll try the orange."

"We have Washington, sir."

The ambassador took the radio microphone from the table. "Hello, this is Ambassador Ralston Dermott," he said loudly. "Whom am I talking to?" Somewhere along the triangular path

210

from Tehran to satellite to Washington a series of clicks answered him. Then came a surprisingly clear voice in return.

"Ralston, this is Emmanuel Holachek. Is this a scrambled circuit?"

The communications technician nodded. "Yes, Emmanuel."

"What's the situation?"

"It looks critical from here. I've found out that the man named David Bass has an Iranian girlfriend named Zhaleh Hekmat. That's Zhaleh with a *zh* as in Jacques. She's listed in the files of the Ministry of Culture and Art as a suspected member of the Muslim Marxist Alliance. Apparently her family is too important for her to be arrested. She also studied in the States. As for Bass, he works for the outfit that holds a maintenance contract for the Shah's personal helicopters. We also have notification that the Shah plans to make an unannounced flight to Nishapur tomorrow afternoon. Nishapur is where my man Quintana disappeared; and he may have radioed from there. I think it all adds up to a bomb in the helicopter."

"That's what it looks like from here too, Ralston. The connection with the Hekmat woman was missed during Bass's security check. CIA has just confirmed it."

"I can telephone the maintenance company and have him pulled off the job immediately, or else I can call SAVAK. How do you want me to do it? If I go to the Iranians, we might never get our hands on Bass; but if I don't tell them first, they're sure to raise hell over it."

There was a long pause. "Who's in the room with you, Ralston?"

"A technician."

"Send him out."

The technician promptly took off his earphones and left the room.

"Okay, Emmanuel, go ahead."

"Listen to this carefully, Ralston." The disembodied voice had taken on a harsh quality. "I have spoken to the President. He has decided that it is the policy of the United States not to

211

intervene in the internal affairs of Iran. Did you get that? Not to intervene."

The set of the ambassador's jaw hardened. "Clarification. Are the actions of an American private citizen working in Iran for an American company considered an internal Iranian affair?"

"They are."

"I can't agree with that decision, Emmanuel."

"It's a presidential decision."

"Does the President realize that this means the Shah will go down?"

"The President is fully aware of the possible consequences of his decision, Ralston. The decision has been approved by the National Security Council. It is up to the Shah to save the Shah."

"I want to have this in writing, Emmanuel. I will also send you a written protest."

"You'll have written confirmation within the hour. It will say that our policy is nonintervention. I wanted to make sure personally that you knew what the policy meant. That's all I have to say, Ralston. Keep me continuously informed of what happens. The next week may be a difficult one for all of us. Goodbye, Ralston. Good luck."

"Good-bye, Emmanuel."

The circuit clicked dead. A low hum issued from the radio speaker. Oblivious of the sound, Ralston Dermott leaned on the table full of electronic instruments and gazed at a calendar tacked to a bulletin board. A feeling of fullness rose in his throat. It was the feeling of incipient tears. He had not felt it in years. He choked it down and turned to see the technician gazing at him through the soundproof window of the room.

David Bass arose unusually early for his eight-o'clock shift. He had slept poorly. He had lain in bed for hours rehearsing the plan that should see him safely airborne on his way to Beirut by the time the Shah was scheduled to touch down in Nishapur. It was a simple plan: no more than feigning a headache to leave work early, grabbing a taxi to the airport, and boarding Air

France No. 308. But the imponderables rolled through his mind as he stared at the dark ceiling. What if he couldn't find a taxi? Would there be a traffic jam? Would the flight be on time? Then an overriding question thrust itself into his mind and would not let go. Would Zhaleh join him in Beirut as she had promised? Toward morning he dozed for an hour but wakened with a start at the sound of a bird singing near his window.

CHAPTER 31

The crow of a distant rooster awakened Mohammad Hormozi from pill-induced sleep. The feel of satin sheets and the pastel elegance of the bedroom seemed momentarily unfamiliar. Then he remembered the place and the day and the ordeal ahead. He ate with methodical slowness the large breakfast brought by a servant, as if he could force upon himself a deliberate calm that would carry him through the next few hours. He removed his white mulla's robe and turban from the closet where he had placed them upon his arrival. After some experimenting he found that the revolver he had brought could be held securely at his side by the knotted white sash that served as a belt. He satisfied himself before a floor-length mirror that the brown outer cloak, despite its open front, would conceal the weapon. He regretted that circumstances had made it impossible to grow a beard. The Twelfth Imam really should have a beard. His last preparation before leaving the guesthouse was to browbeat the servant in charge to give him a duplicate key to the main suite that had already been prepared for the Shah's arrival. It took several increasingly dire threats to break the man's instinctive resistance to the request.

The air was fresh when he finally stepped outside, but thick clouds were lowering over the mountains. He debated between walking to the prayer grounds by way of the Mohammad Mahruq shrine, which was the path the mullas would normally take, and going by way of the gravel road that was already thick with pilgrims. He opted for the latter. It would not be desirable to encounter any of the senior mullas at this particular moment.

Alone and unremarked he made his way with the throng of pilgrims to the huge prayer grounds that suddenly looked small under the load of the swarm of people milling about it. The drama of Hossein Makfuf, which would continue for hours with intermissions for sermons and prayers, was soon to begin, and a group of teen-aged boys dressed like seminary students were struggling to keep the roped-off performance area in front of the great platform free of wandering pilgrims. The platform itself was deserted. Only a lonely microphone on a stand indicated the spot where a succession of sermonizers had harangued the throng the day before and would do so again as the day wore on. On either side of the platform stood the long closed tents in which the women would sit and listen to the sermons.

As Hormozi mounted the low platform in front of the shrine, he saw that a few dignitaries were already present. Immediately his heart lightened, and a smile crossed his face for the first time since the cock's crow. He moved in the direction of the highest-ranking dignitary, the mayor of Nishapur, and set about plying the politician's trade. All thought of what the afternoon would bring mercifully faded away in a sea of mutual compliments and formal introductions.

Behind the notables' platform in the shrine of Hossein Makfuf, the diminutive custodian was quivering with excitement. The rumor had spread the day before like a cascading chain reaction that the Shah was coming personally to dedicate the shrine. Most of the pilgrims he had talked to were too bewildered by the press of thousands of people or too absorbed in their own religious emotions to contemplate what such a visit might mean or where the rumor had started, but the custodian had eventually been able to determine that the source of the rumor had been servants at the Shah's guesthouse at Omar Khayyam. Reassured by the apparent authenticity of the source, he had been dreaming ever since of the magnificent shrine that the Shah would undoubtedly build to the blessed saint Hossein Makfuf. As he gazed at the four drab, whitewashed walls of the tiny building he was now in, his mind's eye saw great ogival archways covered with turquoise-blue tile; and the small white hemisphere over his head became transformed into a great celestial expanse crisscrossed by rays of light from latticed windows, rays of sunlight that picked out the ornate calligraphy on the inner curves of the exquisitely pointed dome.

The sound of a sermon being boomed out over the overwhelming public address system drew his attention back to reality. He climbed the ladder to the small aperture in the dome from which he could see what was happening in the prayer grounds over the top of the green awning that sheltered the heads of the dignitaries on the platform. Consulting his script and studying the stilted movements of the brightly costumed actors in the performance area, he determined that all was on schedule and that the father of Hossein Makfuf was about to be martyred in a particularly gruesome way. He climbed back down and undid a piece of cloth in which he had wrapped a sheaf of parchment-like leaves of bread and a rough ball of white goat cheese. His own part would not come for several hours.

Milling in the crowd itself not far from the southern end of the great platform was Jamshid Ansari. He was carrying a rough hemp sack and, in order to blend into the anonymous mass, had donned a cheap black suit purchased in the bazaar. His pointed white Italian shoes drew occasional curious looks, but the growing intensity of the drama had brought such looks to an end. All around him were sounds of weeping and murmured prayers as

216

the devotees gave free rein to their emotions in sympathy with the tragic family of Hossein Makfuf. The dismemberment of his brother Yahya had just been enacted with a profuse outpouring of artificial blood, and now a sermon was being preached on the moral lesson of the pitiful event.

The people who had brought food with them had discreetly consumed their lunches in covert bites and swallows an hour or so before, but the great majority of the throng would not eat until the drama was completed in the evening. Jamshid looked at his watch. It was three o'clock. He began to make his way toward the opening that separated the women's tents from the platform and gave access to the platform's rear.

For the dignitaries a small buffet had been provided beyond popular view beneath their awning. Very few were paying the least attention to the drama being acted out before them. Mohammad Hormozi had been nervously gregarious throughout the morning and had made a point, because of his religious garb, of occasionally attending to the sermons and the play. A few bites from the buffet had warned him that his stomach would tolerate nothing in it. He had set three-fifteen as the time for moving into position. As the hour approached, his mouth went dry and his speaking was reduced to a few words and to nervous nods and shakes of the head. On the point of three-fifteen he murmured a vague excuse to a member of the governor's staff and left the platform.

At three-thirty Jamshid was standing at the spot where the path from the Mohammad Mahruq shrine terminated and the stairway climbing the back of the platform commenced. A loudspeaker conveyed the voices of the actors behind the platform, but the solid rear wall prevented any sight of the action. Consequently, there were only a few people sitting on the ground listening and a larger number passing back and forth bound on nameless errands. Dr. Hormozi was nowhere to be seen. Several times Jamshid had reached into his cloth sack and fingered the submachine gun contained within. It was cocked and the safety released. In the distance he could see a group of people moving slowly down the path from the shrine. In the front he could make out a man with a large staff.

Perched on his ladder looking out over the green awning of the dignitaries' stand, the custodian of the Hossein Makfuf shrine was following the progress of the lugubrious drama and checking it against his script. The blind martyr's hands and feet had already been cut off and a long demonic speech delivered by the vile commander of the soldiers who were torturing him. The moans of the massed audience were growing ever louder. The women's high-pitched wails could be heard over everything despite the muffling of their tents. Soon the head of Hossein Makfuf would be cut off, and another vilely triumphant speech would be delivered by the godless military commander. After that the custodian's eyes would be fixed on the great empty platform, for there would appear another actor portraying Hossein Makfuf praying in paradise. The moment he appeared the custodian would close the switch that would turn on the glorious lights of paradise, mounted on beams extending across the platform.

Pressed in the thick of the worshipful mass of pilgrims Mohammad Hormozi heard the immense moan of thousands of voices as the head was hacked off the manikin portraying Hossein Makfuf. His heart was pounding, and he felt on the verge of screaming. The crowd would not give away for him. He was near the end of the platform, but the minutes were flying past. He pushed and tugged at body after body, but the spirit of lamentation had taken hold so strongly that his efforts to advance were scarcely noticed. His arms were tired. He felt as if he were trying to swim to keep from drowning while the water got thicker and thicker. One thought drummed in his mind: The opportunity will never recur in our lifetimes.

Suddenly a space appeared before him. Four young men were straining to create some room for him. One of them shouted to him above the din of lamentation.

"Hurry! We're with Jamshid! We saw your turban!"

Forcefully the four bodyguards bulled their way through the

weeping and oblivious crowd. Briefly the shadow of the women's tent blocked the low western sun, and then the crowd abruptly thinned as they passed the corner of the great platform. Moving at a stately pace, the blind mulla with his heavy staff was about fifty meters down the path. His eyes seemed to be focused on a distant horizon. Following in his footsteps was a company of other mullas led by one whom Hormozi recognized as Ayatollah Pirzadeh. On the opposite side of the path from Hormozi stood Jamshid Ansari with his hand inside the rough hemp sack. One of Hormozi's protectors ran over to him and spoke into his ear. Jamshid made a quick glance in the minister's direction. Hormozi felt nervously for the outline of the revolver under his cloak. At the same time he sensed a strange calm beginning to come over him.

The vainglorious rants of the murderer of Hossein Makfuf were reaching a deafening crescendo over the public address system. High on his distant ladder the shrine custodian eagerly fingered his switch as he gazed intently through the tiny aperture. The wails and groans of the crowd pounded louder and louder on his ears.

When the distance narrowed to five meters Jamshid pulled the submachine gun from the sack and stepped calmly to the middle of the path. At his shouted command the train of mullas came to a jumbled halt. Only the blind man continued his stately pace, his lips moving in prayer. Hands were prodding Hormozi toward the staircase, but he was riveted by the sight. Now Pirzadeh was gesturing and there were several men with drawn guns running past the cowed line of mullas. Jamshid slowly retreated before the blind man's advance.

Hormozi started to move toward the stairway. He saw a gun in the hand of one of the youths who had helped him through the crowd. As his foot touched the bottom step there was a single shot. The responding cries were absorbed in the wailing din of lamentation. He ran halfway up to a prolonged burst of shooting and paused to look back. The blind mulla was collapsing on the path, his staff cut in half by the bullets of Jamshid's gun. His pristine white gown was spotted with spreading blood. Farther behind Hormozi glimpsed brown robes running away and others laid out in the dirt. Jamshid seemed to be shouting at him, but he could hear nothing but wailing and groaning. He ran up the last remaining steps. As he emerged onto the platform, the gleeful custodian threw his switch.

The roar of a huge explosion eclipsed the cries and moans. Flame spurted forth from beneath the platform and with it flew great chunks of earth and rubble. The actors in front of the platform were lost in a cloud of smoke and dust. More smoke and dust shot skyward through the open spaces in the floor at the ends of the platform. To either side the nearest tent was blown away and the sheltered women pelted by flying bricks and debris. Far across the prayer grounds the green awning covering the opposite platform ballooned upward but did not fall.

Alone on top of the platform Mohammad Hormozi felt barely a tremble underfoot. Possessed by a manic calmness, he stepped to the microphone and raised his arms. He was oblivious of the screams and cries of pain that were beginning to fill the stunned silence. In a magnificent thundering voice he began to speak.

CHAPTER **32**

In the name of God, the merciful, the compassionate. There is no other God but He, and Mohammad is His messenger. God alone is the creator and the master of the day of judgment. God, the all powerful, the victorious, has established for you a guide to the day of judgment. I am he whom God has sent! I am the Mahdi! I am the Twelfth Imam whose return is awaited! Know well that I have come to purge the earth of evil. To kill the beast. To bring the right order. (A fluttering sound began to be heard over the thundering voice and the screams of the wounded.) *Even now does God, the vigilant, the all-seeing, empower me to destroy the beast. Even now does the one who calls himself Shah suffer under my hand.* (Beyond the platform a large sausage-shaped helicopter with imperial markings was descending toward the monument of Omar Khayyam.) *See how the false Shah comes to do battle with God! See how God shall destroy him!* (The turbaned figure on the platform turned and raised his arms in the direction of the fragile machine hovering in the distance. A minute passed. Save for the cries of

221

pain, an unearthly quiet sat upon the vast throng. Suddenly a spot of orange flame appeared on the helicopter's side. In an instant the helicopter disintegrated and began to fall to earth in pieces. A great moan arose from the throat of the crowd. The figure turned around.) *It is God's will! I am God's will! Verily, I am the Twelfth Imam!*

Slowly Hormozi backed away from the microphone. His eyes were fixed in an unfocused stare. He couldn't remember what he had just finished saying, but he knew nevertheless what had happened. The need to turn toward the stairs brought him out of his mesmerized state. Screams and cries now reached his awareness for the first time, and above them a rising swell of prayer and lamentation. He saw the backs of thousands of pilgrims prostrated in prayer, but others were beginning to spew forth from the prayer grounds. He must keep ahead of the crush.

At the bottom of the stairs Jamshid Ansari was waiting with an ashen face. Ten or more bodies lay strewn on the ground. There was a large red stain on the heel of one of his dusty white shoes.

"I've sent the others to the shrine to help Zhaleh." His voice sounded weak. "I think I can make my speech if I can get up the stairs. I've been shot in the foot. You go on to the guesthouse and make the broadcast. Zhaleh will join you when she has finished at the shrine."

Hormozi stared for a moment into the pain-filled face of the young Marxist. Then he nodded. On the path in front of him was the lifeless body of the blind mulla. The sightless eyes still seemed fixed on an unseen horizon. Shortly beyond was a second brown-robed corpse. Beside it on the path was an unbroken pair of glasses with heavy black frames. Hormozi sidestepped the bodies and hurried down the path in the direction of the shrine of Mohammad Mahruq. Behind him Jamshid Ansari was hobbling painfully up the stairs.

A short distance north of the path, but totally obscured from view by the craggy landscape of ruins, Ben Groves cautiously raised his head above the rim of the pit. There was nothing to see but rubble and potsherds. He drew himself out of the hole and reached back to help Frank Quintana over the edge. Just before the great explosion they had heard the running footsteps of their guards and seen their shadows disappear from the side of the pit. Then had come the explosion followed by what had sounded like an amplified sermon of the sort they had been hearing for two days, followed by a second smaller explosion. Then had come silence, and they had started their climb.

Once they had cleared the surface, it took a minute or two to get their bearings. In the direction of the Hossein Makfuf shrine a great cloud of dust was dissipating high in the sky. Once again the amplified sound of a harangue reached their ears. In the opposite direction, beyond the clean outline of the Omar Khayyam monument, a column of black smoke angled toward the mountains in the light breeze. The shrine of Mohammad Mahruq was surprisingly close, close enough so that they could hear sounds of machine-gun fire coming from within the garden walls.

"The warning didn't work," said Ben Groves blankly. There were tears in Frank Quintana's eyes. "Let's try to make it into town."

Steering as straight a path as possible through the ruins, they made for the monument of Omar Khayyam. In the distance on their left and their right they could see increasingly numerous clusters of people going down the gravel road leading from the prayer grounds and the pathway leading to Mohammad Mahruq.

At the wall screening the Omar Khayyam garden from the ruins they would have had to detour around toward the shrine or toward the gravel road. Instead they took a few minutes and piled up a two-foot-high mound of bricks and rubble. Standing on top of it their heads and shoulders were above the level of the wall. Staring back at them from the other side was the grim face of an Iranian with a submachine gun.

As Hormozi passed Mohammad Mahruq the sounds of gunfire were becoming more sporadic. The slaughter of the mullas seemed to be nearing its end. He saw no one on the short stretch of road between the shrine and the guesthouse. Some distance away off the left side of the road lay the smoking wreckage of the Shah's helicopter. Hormozi's gun was drawn, but no servants appeared to question his access to the guesthouse. With an unsteady hand he unlocked the door to the Shah's suite.

Shutting the door behind him, he switched on the crystal chandelier in the spacious foyer. Judging from the placement of the antenna on the roof, he picked the door on the left as the most likely one to lead him to the communications equipment. It passed through his mind that the door might be locked, but it swung open easily at his touch.

Seated on a pink silk sofa facing the door was the Shah of Iran. Standing slightly to the side was Colonel Rahmatollah Ziya. He was holding a gun trained on Hormozi. A half-dozen other army officers were standing along the sides of the room. The Minister of Culture and Art dropped his pistol to the carpet.

"I thought you might come here, Hormozi," said the Shah with a nod of welcome. "Won't you sit down? It's a breach of protocol, but you look as though you are feeling faint." The speechless Hormozi collapsed into the deep feather cushion of a pink armchair. "I wanted to see this continue to the end. It was the only way to find out who was involved. I must admit I admire your courage in carrying out this incredibly foolish act. It was your misfortune that Colonel Ziya came across your name in the notes of an American professor. I do not understand why you told the professor these plans."

"I told him nothing," came the scarcely audible voice of Hormozi.

"Perhaps it was your accomplices, then. No matter. By now they are all killed or captured. I am told that one of them was a very brave woman. It is unfortunate that she could not be taken alive. You may also be interested to know that the young man making the speech chose to kill himself. So you are all alone. Do you have any questions before you too are killed?"

Hormozi was trembling uncontrollably in his chair.

"Possibly you would like to know about the helicopter. That was a surprise. Colonel Ziya advised me, as a precaution, not to follow the plan of travel that you had laid out; but we had not expected a bomb. I regret the loss of the pilot. He was going to fly me back to Tehran. Any other questions?" Hormozi was on the verge of falling from the chair. "If not, you may do your duty, Ziya."

Five bullets ripped through the brown cloak of the Minister of Culture and Art, throwing him back against the cushioned upholstery. His head slumped forward loosely, revealing a dark red stain on the pink silk.

"Now, my dear Colonel," continued the Shah as the echo of the gunshots died, "there is one further matter."

"Your Majesty?" said the elderly colonel questioningly.

"You have spent a lifetime in loyal service to my father and myself, Colonel. I appointed you to the Inspectorate of SAVAK because of that loyalty. Yet the plot you uncovered—and for the second time I owe my life to your vigilance—could not have been created by this poor thing alone." He gestured toward the lifeless body of Mohammad Hormozi. "Nor could it have gone as far as it did without the collaboration of SAVAK. I am left with the unfortunate conclusion, Colonel, that you warned me of the plot only because it had gone wrong. What went wrong and what was originally planned I do not know; but I have a sad feeling that you were a party to it."

The white-mustached colonel bowed deeply from the waist. "I have always been loyal to Your Imperial Majesty and to God the Almighty and his Prophet Mohammad."

"I believe you have one shot remaining in your revolver, Colonel. You may leave the room if you wish."

Colonel Ziya bowed again. "Your Majesty," he said with dignity. He backed respectfully to the door of the foyer and left the room. A single shot rang out. A minute later a junior officer was brought into the Shah's presence.

"What is it?" asked the Shah testily.

"We have captured two Americans, Your Majesty," said the officer. "One is a university professor; the other is from the American embassy."

A smile stretched across the Shah's face. "Bring them to me."

The shock of being led into the presence of the Shah after an hour of questioning and manhandling left Ben Groves and Frank Quintana totally bewildered. The Shah seemed pleased to see them.

"Are you the one who wrote about Dr. Hormozi in your notes?" he asked Groves in carefully enunciated English.

"Yes, Your Majesty. It was only a deduction from various pieces of evidence."

"A clever deduction. A very clever deduction. But it is also possible that you were part of the plot, is it not? If you were in my position trying to make a deduction from, as you say, various pieces of evidence, would you not come to that conclusion?"

"We did everything in our power to warn you, Your Majesty," replied Frank Quintana. "I radioed the warning about the helicopter to the American embassy."

"I received no warning about the helicopter."

Frank once again looked bewildered. "I know it was received, Your Majesty," he said weakly.

"I regret very much that your deaths may cause an international incident, but I seem to be left with no other choice. It will seem . . ."

"Your Majesty," interrupted Groves abruptly, "I have a suggestion I wish to make before you make a final decision."

"You may proceed," said the Shah.

CHAPTER **33**

"Have you seen this cable from Ralston Dermott?" said Emmanuel Holachek to his special assistant for Middle Eastern affairs.

Bill Keller nodded. "I don't know quite what to make of it."

"Seems straightforward enough. The Shah is going to announce that his son has been revealed by God to be the Twelfth Imam. This will be announced throughout the country in all of the mosques on the tenth day of Moharram. That Minister of Culture and Art, it seems, will be declared the Antichrist, who had to be destroyed before the true Messiah could appear."

"It just seems incredible," said Keller, shaking his head. "The Shah isn't even a member of the right family to produce the Twelfth Imam."

"I presume God has fixed that up, too. From a policy point of view, this makes for a pretty good result, wouldn't you say?"

"I expect it does. Should take care of the succession problem, at least. I just wonder if the people will buy it."

"Strange part of the world," mused Holachek. "I suppose now

it's time to get back to the Arabs and the Israelis."

"The Assistant Secretary has scheduled Quintana's debriefing for tomorrow morning. I think I'll stop by. He might know who thought up the idea of the Shah's son being the Twelfth Imam. Do you still think it was a bad idea to send Quintana out there?"

"Terrible idea."

"By the way, David Bass has been taken into custody in Beirut. He had registered in a hotel as Mr. and Mrs. David and Zhaleh Bass. Apparently he was just sitting in his room waiting for his girlfriend to arrive from Iran when they found him."

At the end of Moharram it was announced that Professor Benjamin Groves would become the first Hidden Imam Professor of Iranian Culture. The rumor in academic circles was that the chair was endowed to the tune of two million dollars by the Shah of Iran himself.

Afterword

The tombstone around which this story is built actually exists, unnoticed, beside the railroad track in the ruins of Nishapur. It's physical condition and appearance are just as described. What relation it may have to the actual historical figure of Hossein Makfuf remains an open question. The hypothesis that it is a partial copy of an original stone destroyed in the excavating of the railroad right-of-way is unsubstantiated. An Iranian historian and religious authority who has been consulted on the matter is of the opinion that the stone is a fraud perpetrated, in all likelihood, by someone who may have claimed that Hossein Makfuf came to him in a dream and pointed out his last resting place, which was then duly marked with a small monument. The beneficiary of the dream was presumably rewarded for his pious vision. This hypothesis too is unsubstantiated; but frauds of this sort are not unknown in Iran.

Many questions remain, perhaps never to be answered. Why is the inscription on the stone so garbled and badly carved? Arabic words are confused with Persian words. Names are misspelled or given in defective or incomplete forms. Why is the name given for Hossein Makfuf's mother different from that preserved in medieval texts? The name on the stone is that of the mother of Hossein's brother Yahya; his own mother is reported to have been a slave girl. Why, if it is a recently concocted pious fraud, is the stone so little noticed by the citizens of Nishapur?

Questions aside, whether fraudulent or genuine, this stone or another, the appearance of a catalyst for transforming religious expectation of the Twelfth Imam's reappearance into political action is always a possibility in Iranian Islam. It has happened in the past; it can happen again. No government is immune to destruction by this means.

Save for the prologue, this story was written in entirety in the summer of 1978, prior to the major street demonstrations that marked the beginning of the Iranian revolution. Since then the political order in Iran has been entirely overturned. The Shah has been overthrown and an Islamic Republic proclaimed. What the future will bring to that still politically turbulent country remains uncertain. However, the religious, social, and political viewpoints described in this book have not gone away. They will continue to influence the course of events just as surely as the Hidden Imam will one day reappear to usher in the millenium.